Wrinkles in MEMORY

“Debalina’s writing brings back vivid memories for every reader. There are morsels for everyone in *Wrinkles in Memory*. Her expressive writing style immerses you in the short passages. Keeps the pages turning.”

– *Parag Saigaonkar, Author*

“The many women Debalina is, is so evident in these stories. They are so heart-warming, poignant, funny, and thought-provoking that they are pretty unputdownable.”

– *Neelam Kumar, Author and Motivational Speaker*

“Poignant and sensitive portrayal of real life musings. A delightful read...unexpected endings leave you waiting for (and wanting) more.”

– *Prof. Payal Mehra, IIM Lucknow*

Wrinkles in MEMORY

Debalina Haldar

LiFi Publications Pvt. Ltd.
New Delhi

Published by:
LiFi Publications Pvt. Ltd.
211, 2nd Floor, Gagandeep
12, Rajendra Place, New Delhi–110 008, India
Phone : (011) 2574 1000
E-mail : info@lifipublications.com
Web : www.lifipublications.com

ISBN 13: 978-93-82536-26-0 ISBN 10: 93-82536-26-4

First published in 2016

Cataloging in Publication Data—DK
[Courtesy: D.K. Agencies (P) Ltd. <docinfo@dkagencies.com>]

Haldar, Debalina, 1989– **author.**
Wrinkles in memory / Debalina Haldar.
pages cm
Short stories.
ISBN 9789382536260

1. Haldar, Debalina, 1989- --Childhood and youth--Fiction.
2. Short stories, Indic (English) I. Title.

PR9499.4.H35W75 2016 DDC 823.92 23

Printed in India by D.K. Fine Art Press (P) Ltd., Delhi–52

'In good and bad times you've always been there to count on,

In happy and sad times you've always been there to turn to,

Whatever life has brought, you've always been there with your selfless love.'

This book has been dedicated to my parents.

Contents

Foreword

I came to know Debalina Haldar, the author of this book, when I was employed by Thames River Press, to be the developmental editor of her novel, *The Female Ward*. I had been involved with the publisher through my editing work with Indira Chandrasekhar on our anthology, *Pangea, an Anthology of Stories from Around the Globe*. Both of these books are now with Thames River Press's sister imprint, Union Bridge Books. The early version of *The Female Ward* was certainly intriguing, but the book had quite a way to go before it could be considered a finished and publishable manuscript. So we worked on it with gusto, and once we came to know each other's methods and ways of thinking, we worked very well together. When we had completed the project, I know I missed working with Ms Haldar, and I remember that time now with fondness. We never met in person; everything we achieved took place online, and we didn't communicate through Skype. So it was a tremendous pleasure for me to be able to meet her in Mumbai in January of 2013.

I read the stories in *Wrinkles in Memory* with great interest, as writing the short story is a very different craft to that of writing novels, and being a short story writer myself, I have a critical eye for the quality of short stories. Although no two stories in this collection are alike – each can stand alone – they are bound together through the theme of reminiscence. Perhaps for that very reason, the collection includes many fond stories, some stories of regret, and some of loss. One of the writing skills Ms Haldar shows in this collection is that she can create a smooth transition from past events or memories back into the present time – a very necessary skill in a set of stories based around the theme of memory.

Overall, this is a balanced collection and one in which the author's compassion and well as her ability to acutely observe is well demonstrated. Some of the stories are sentimental, and often Ms Haldar's strong feeling against injustice and inequality in her society is clearly shown. One of the characteristics of her writing is that she can write about sad or unfortunate situations but very often ends a story on a note of hope. She is not afraid to tackle serious issues directly, as in the poignant, prize-winning story, *Shackles of the Night Sky*, which was her response to learning about the 1994 genocide in Rwanda. Or, *The Empty Title*, in which a beggar child and a wealthy young woman have in common the fact that they both have hard finger tips, the beggar child from a life of poverty, and the young woman because she is a musician who plays a guitar.

Although the stories themselves are not over-burdened with extraneous matter, Ms Haldar has a fine eye for small detail. I was particularly struck by a line about Mumbai in *The Blue Sky Steps* in which Mumbai is 'a land with hidden sky, detached moon and aloof trees.' Not only is the sentence succinct, but it is arrestingly memorable and shows her grasp of things poetic. This particular story is one of several sweet and sad tales of loss and growing up. Another such is, *The Old Giant*, which although a sad story, has a terrific ending. And again, I was in admiration of this passage: 'The part of the sari was a beautiful maze of golden threads, little glass pieces and sequins. There was a very narrow space between the threads and sequins for the cloth to breathe. It was his mother's, he recalled.'

Another element of Ms Haldar's work that I am drawn to is her descriptive writing. Most, if not all of these stories have, even if only in a handful of words, passages about the sun, the colours in nature, the effects of wind – and her descriptions of the natural world often lends atmosphere and sometimes drama to her stories. So in *The Old Giant*: 'Sunlight seeped diamond-shaped through the leaves of the trees that lined the Thakurnagar Hospital.'

As well as beauty and gentleness, Ms Haldar can turn her hand to sinister stories such as *When the Trunk Creaks* which has tantalisingly little backstory within it, but it is this very fact, I think, that lends weight to its darkness. The story is told in the first person through the eyes of a male character and is testimony to the fact that Ms Haldar is able to write male as well as female characters convincingly. Indeed, part of a writer's work is to become practised in writing from the point of view of the other gender so that the reader believes in the character. Again, in *Stubborn*, another story with a good ending, the main character is a man struggling with his broken marriage. In this story, it would seem that the couple did not heed the advice of her mother who said, "...that little things in relationships fuse into one another, and form something like huge, big boulders that can no longer be removed."

I see Ms Haldar as a true romantic writer in the old sense of that word where 'romantic' does not relate only to lovers. A number of her characters, the very poor ones most particularly, have some of the heroic qualities found in old romances. *By-lane Dreamers*, another award-winning story, is about two boys from the slums who work to make enough money to go to Nicco leisure park. But as no one else will get into the toy boat they are in on the lake – to complete the set of four passengers needed – the manager, not believing they have legitimate tickets, gets a guard to throw them out of the park.

Perhaps the most heroic of Ms Haldar's characters living in poverty are to be found in *Little Crayons at the Black Gate* in which Raju and her older sister, Deepali, who live in a roadside shack made from sheets of plastic, do not feel they are entitled to new crayons: '...children in school have better bigger newer crayons. We can have the smaller used ones.'

As if to throw into relief the stories about poor people, this collection includes *The All-Rounder*, about how being rich doesn't necessarily make you happy – how obsession with money, or 'financial intoxication' can make you forget what your children need from you. In conclusion, there is much in this collection to stir the reader into thoughtfulness, and I hope to see Ms Haldar go from strength to strength in her writing over the years.

Rebecca Lloyd
World Fantasy Award nominee
and winner of the New Fictions Prize 2016

Author's Note

I have a terrible memory and I do not remember much. But I do remember, when I was eleven years old I was sitting in our garden and I had a diary where I was writing. Years later, now, I realise how it had sowed the seed of what I was going to do later. The poem goes back a long time – to the year 2000 and it is not a very good poem. But I'd still like to share it here. It said:

I woke up and saw a rainbow today,
A rainbow with colours so many,
The blue and orange and yellow and green,
Yet not praised enough, not any.
I'd like to see a fading red,
Or a golden striking new,
A shimmery silver ruling the sky,
Or a simple, sober blue.
Until the day I rule the sky,
I'd try to reach up high,
And if I try to reach up high,
I may just skim the sky.

I feel very lucky that at the age of eleven I kind of knew what I was going to do and in retrospect I can now connect the dots. This poem was published in *The Telegraph*, a widely read newspaper in Kolkata in the same year.

This is my second book after my debut novel, *The Female Ward.*

Writing has been an enriching experience for me. It is soothing, the most comforting pat on the shoulder in times of distress. And I must confess here that this is a never ending journey for me – not only for my own comfort, but as a strong medium for encouraging a healthy process of constructive thinking among my readers.

I have always been fascinated by the idea of short stories. The most delightful part of short stories is their impact albeit the length. A larger part of my childhood was spent in Kolkata and hence, the stories are mostly rooted to the aristocratic city of joy. However, in the later years, I moved to Mumbai where my parents live now and likewise, few stories in the anthology originate in Mumbai.

I must take this opportunity to write about 'Shackles of the Night Sky', set in the African country, Rwanda. I learnt about the genocide and the war between the Hutus and the Tutsis and was highly moved by the unbelievable numbers that statistics showed. 'Shackles of the Night Sky' is the story of a Tutsi woman who takes care of a Hutu child in the wake of the Rwandan genocide. This story was given the 1st Prize in IIM Bangalore's Annual Entrepreneurship Summit, Eximius, which had the theme, 'The Road Less Taken'.

A couple of other stories in this collection have received awards. 'By-lane Dreamers' was given the Critics' Choice Award by Illuminati 2011. Illuminati is an annual short story writing competition organized by manipalblog.com and runs across the country. The competition had the theme, 'Like a moth to the flame'. 'Little Crayons at the Back Gate' had won the short story competition Anubhuti in 2014. It was organized by an NGO called Sarthak Foundation at the Lucknow Literary Fest and ran across India.

'The Last Meeting' is a story by a guest author. Debakanya Haldar is my younger sister, currently studying M.A. in English at Jawaharlal Nehru University. She did her B.A. in English from St. Xavier's College, Kolkata. She gives a touching description of a tender love story.

Think about your brain. What perhaps comes to the mind is a two-lobed, roundish, grey mass with lots of wrinkles, formed by experiences and memories. I sincerely hope the journey through this book would create lots of amazing memories for my readers. Hence, I call this book, *Wrinkles in Memory.*

Happy reading.

Debalina Haldar

Acknowledgement

I take this opportunity to thank my parents and sisters for supporting me always like really strong, gigantic pillars. My heartfelt gratitude to Aritro for always being there and most significantly, being assertive of my capabilities. Without his support this book would have never been created. I would like to give special thanks to all my professors, and teachers for their wishes to see this book published. A special acknowledgement to all my well-wishers whose presence had a profound impact on the completion of this book.

Rebecca Lloyd, author of multiple novels and short stories, has always been there by my side with her significant guidance. I am indebted to her for providing me the first lessons in the intricacies of fiction writing.

Dida, my grandmother, had a deep impact on me throughout my life. Her strong knowledge of poems, stories and novels by Tagore and Sarat Chandra Chatterjee largely influenced my taste for books. Had she lived to see this book she would have been extremely happy.

And last but not the least, I would thank LiFi Publications and the entire team for this book.

This is a work of fiction. However, given the number of snippets presented, a reader must be in close proximity to at least one of them. And if any snippet is in close proximity to infinite such readers, then it must be true to all of them. Hence, it may not be entirely fictional as I had thought.

1

The Paper Boat

We've had this old and faded photograph with us for a number of years in our family photo album. It is the picture of my maternal grandfather. I remember my grandmother quite well because a larger part of my childhood was spent in her house in Thakurnagar after she had been widowed. I used to be very fond of her and can recall that I enjoyed her special affection for me over my cousins.

In the photograph, my grandfather is seated in a chair, at the bottom of the long steps of our small cottage in Chittaranjan, where we lived then. He has me in his arms and I think I must have been merely one or two months old. We were there in the shadows thrown by a large coconut tree which is not in the picture. I can tell it was a coconut tree by seeing the crown of the pinnately compound long fronds. The picture had turned yellow over the years and there is a spot of damp at the corner.

My grandfather was a slim, trim man. He didn't keep a drooping moustache like most men of his age did in the late 1980s and early 1990s. My mother tells me that he had a strong personality. He looked unwell in the photo. When I looked into his eyes in the photograph I was immediately struck by the confidence that radiated out of them.

There isn't much detail that I remember about my grandfather. He died when I was five years old. Someone had called up to give the news of his demise and the following day I left with my mother to see him for the last time.

I have the nitty-gritty of my grandfather's house fresh in mind. It was huge and covered a great part of land by the pond that was behind it. I reached the place with my mother for his funeral. It was in the month of July and the air had the sweet smell of wet mud. I remember the tall trees and the fresh air distinctly of that place. Every time I visited Thakurnagar, I felt a strong connection with the trees that lined the narrow road. Whenever the trees saw me, they moved as if to turn in my direction.

A strong wind was blowing and it felt really very cold and seemed so unfamiliar and bizarre. But the trees remembered me. They bowed gently in the breeze...and called me nearer, welcoming me.

We walked past the pond. I don't remember seeing the water level higher than that ever. The water was clear and reflected the large, evergreen, spirally arranged leaves at the top of the stems of the palm trees. The wind was gone and it was all silent again. The ducks communicated by loud and sharp scaups. While some shy ones made quieter contact calls. They all gathered near the pond.

As soon as I entered the house the smell of sandalwood had intoxicated me. I went into a state of trance. There was a huge photo of my grandfather in the main hall with garlands around it and many people inside the house...I don't remember seeing most of them again. But what I remember very clearly till date is my grandfather's inanimate form...his eyes closed, sandalwood dots on the forehead, his body covered in a large white cloth, showing his feet. There were two tiny cotton balls inside his nostrils. He looked so peaceful that day, free of every tension, every confusion in the world. I had never seen anyone like that before. My mind was filled with questions. I understood that that wasn't the right time to ask. I had never seen my mother cry the way she did that day. She hugged my grandfather for a long time before someone made her sit back. I stood at the corner of the hall, obviously shocked. I felt like crying too.

I looked across the hall. My grandmother was sitting at the other end, near the wall. She covered her face with both her hands. I couldn't make out if she was crying. I couldn't see her face. As I looked around the room I saw few familiar faces...I chose to let everyone mourn and kept my questions with me. I don't think I knew then what death meant. This I remember because of Gokul Kaka and what he had told me the following day. Gokul Kaka had been my grandfather's neighbour for many years.

Someone took me inside, I can't remember who. I found my cousins there...jolly, unlike the people inside the hall. I doubt if any of them were aware of what had happened to my grandfather. They were all of my age, roughly. They called me inside and we started playing among ourselves. Somehow, I have always found the company of cousins more fascinating than that of friends. We played all day and I forgot about what happened earlier that day inside the hall.

That night I slept beside my mother. I woke up in the middle of the night. She was crying. I didn't call her but stayed awake for hours, I remember, lying by her side, listening to her. I wanted to ask her a lot of things at that hour in the night. Every time I made an attempt, I stopped myself. I kept wondering as the insects made the buzzing noise in the silence of the night...as my mother poured out her heart and wetted the pillow. I noticed a small tear drop forming at the corner of my eyes.

The next morning as soon as the sun peeked through the trees that lined the pond, I woke up. My grandfather's photo was still there in the main hall and there were people always coming in with flower garlands and small packets of sweets. My grandfather was no longer lying on the floor. My cousins were still asleep in another room. I couldn't, bear the burning sensation of my vague concept of things that were happening, anymore. I wanted to leave my mother alone. She was up very early that morning. I ran down the long sky blue steps, past the trees, three pines, a straggling oak and a huge mango. Gokul Kaka was standing against the rough and gnarled trunk of an oak tree. He was a middle-aged short man, who always wore impeccable white trousers and preferred to leave the upper part of his body bare. His hair was greying towards the temples near his forehead and behind his ears. He wore glasses with a thick, black frame. His study was filled with books. I still don't know if he had read them all. He could sing... not very well, but very loud, especially when he took a bath every evening in the pond. He was a great entertainer. Kids loved him for his effortless mimicry of animals and humans even. Once, I can recall, he had mimicked my grandmother and how she used to wake up every morning and complain about the cold water, short winter days, rising prices or about some tenant who used a lot of water the previous day or dirtied the lawn.

I asked him about my grandfather and that I couldn't understand why he was lying like that in the hall the other day. He said that my grandfather was gone into the waters, of ponds and lakes and seas and oceans, and I believed him at once because he was the most credulous person I knew then. He was a nice man and a great story teller. The stories, when combined with his narration, always looked as good as true. I was almost convinced why the water level was higher than ever. I learnt from Gokul

Kaka that those packets and garlands were for my grandfather so that he would return from the waters. I looked towards the way to the pond. I was determined to bring him back.

I ran back home through the lawn. The grass beneath the cherry tree had water at the tip which touched my legs. The sunrays sparkled like diamonds through the leaves of the trees. The main hall now had more people praying over my grandfather to bring him back. I slowly moved inside, to the room where I had kept my bag. I had just learnt how paper boats were made. Our strict art and craft teacher had made me do it ten times before it came out perfectly. I made a small paper boat out of an old newspaper that was lying on the wooden table at the corner of the room near the door. I folded and refolded the newspaper again and again till I was convinced that it was strong enough to sail in the water through wind, rain and turbulent conditions till it reached its destination. It came out beautifully. My teacher would've been proud of me had she seen it. I don't remember having made a better paper boat again. I took out a small paper from my writing pad and wrote in clear bold letters, 'I MISS YOU. COME BACK.' I think this was the first time I'd ever written a letter.

I walked out of the main hall. I made sure that my mother didn't notice me. She was already upset and had lots of work. I was glad that she didn't find me as I sneaked out of the house. The sky had changed its sunny mood by then. The clouds looked like incorrigible monsters, spread all over the sky. My heart began pumping fast, since I had to return before it started raining. I walked fast. I wished I could meet Gokul Kaka on my way. I kept looking around as I walked but couldn't see him anywhere. I reached the pond. The water was calm. I looked at the letter and quickly scribbled the word 'SOON' at the end of my message. I folded the letter and placed it inside the boat. The ducks weren't there. The image of the palm leaves on the water was dull and unclear. It was an unusual day. The leaves were still...the sun had hidden behind the clouds. I looked around. I sailed the boat in the water and watched as it moved away from me. It reached the center of the pond. All of a sudden, a storm rose. I ran to the nearest tree and hugged it tightly. There was dust everywhere and soon some of it went into my eyes. I shut my eyes with my hands. The wind was there for a little while.

After some time, the gushing sound of the wind, the loud bang of window panes, the rubbing noise of the leaves...all of those were gone. And when it was silent again, I rubbed my eyes. I looked for the paper boat in the pond. I couldn't see it! The paper boat wasn't there...it went to my grandfather, perhaps, I thought. I went back to the house before it was late.

I don't usually go through old photos and albums. But now that I did I was glad since I sailed through a sweet memory of my grandfather, a remarkable person I remember so little about.

Of course, I've grown up over the years now. I've seen numerous deaths since the first one. I certainly know what death means now. But the wonderful journey through this memory made me think again. I wonder about the purpose of the wind out of nowhere on a bright and sunny day. I wonder if the paper boat could ever reach him. This might be an insensible thing to expect, I thought, but then who knows what happens after one dies. I closed the album. And as I walked towards my bed at the end of the day, the last puff of the wind brought from the villages the scent of damp mud, and whispered the words into my ears, 'I miss you too.'

2

The Last Meeting

There is something bitterly strange about the lake in Teresa Park. Few years back, when we used to stare into the mist, into the nothingness, we would feel completely whole. Few years later, standing in the same place, I felt completely empty. The water was uncomfortably calm and my vision was blurred with a rush of memories.

'What if the world isn't what we think it is?' he said as he threw a pebble and created a ripple in the middle of the lake.

'What do you mean?'

'I don't want to grow up, Jules. I don't even know why I said that.'

'It's okay. We'll pull through. Together.'

I looked at my watch. Twenty past ten. I grasped the cold rusted railings, took a deep breath and left. That was the first time I had visited the lake all alone and that also was my last time. I never went back there.

I drove past a number of known places – the Cineplex Movie Hall, The Cookie Pie shop and the long lines of small bookstores from where we would usually buy poetry books. As I took a turn, I passed the fair ground. Every winter he would take me there. We would shoot balloons, gorge upon exceptionally sweet pretzels and fool around with the burly old man selling watches. It was also here where I rode the Giant Wheel for the first time.

'Don't tell me that you've never ridden it!'

'I haven't. So? Big deal!'

'No, you're going to ride it tonight! Come on!'

'You're not going to make me do this. No way. I am scared of heights.'

'I'll hold you. Okay?'

'But...but it's scary!'

'I won't let go of you. I promise.'

For the last two winters, however, the story has been different. This time, the fair had been bigger than ever with more stalls and rides. We didn't get to see the splendour, though. It's been more than two years and even though we called each other up now and then, we hardly met. The distance had crept up gradually between us like those invisible cancer cells, ever since we had started working, being busy almost every day.

Anna's return to the city a year back proved to be the catalyst. She is a good-looking, sweet-tempered girl, and I have never met her. We have somehow always managed to evade the topic of Anna. I got to know about her return and the reason for the same from a mutual friend. Anna is his girlfriend and now, his fiancé.

It was five minutes to eleven and I was almost there – The Bulgarian Cafe. I smiled at the thought that I was going to meet him after a long time. But soon enough reality struck me. I was just three blocks away from the cafe and I pulled over and parked the car along the pavement. I stared at all the cars that sped by and my heart sank. I knew that I couldn't do it. I had almost made up my mind about going back home but then I recalled our last phone conversation two nights back.

'Jules?'

'Hey! It's been such a long time! Been busy, eh?'

'Well, yeah, kind of. How are you?'

'Not bad. Doing pretty good.'

There was silence for some time.

'So? What makes you call me so suddenly?' I said.

Silence.

'Umm...I guess you haven't heard it. I'm getting engaged to Anna. This Sunday.'

Silence.

'Oh...' I tried to find words to fill up the disturbing stretch of stillness. 'I'm really happy for you two.'

'Can you meet me this Saturday? At our usual place? I need to see you.'

'Of course, I will.'

The news was not a sudden bolt from the blue. He knew that as well. A part of me had always known about this inevitable day. It had taken up the doleful task of preparing me for this precise moment – "I'm getting engaged" – and every second of my life, even the moments we had spent together, were an unconscious attempt at accepting this truth. But it was always unconscious – I never dared to think of it out loud, never dared to accept it. And now, I was finally facing it all alone.

I stayed put in the car after I'd parked it in front of the cafe, reached for my wallet and took out a tainted photograph. It was taken three years back at the fair. We were both trying to ape the "gangster look" and truly enough, we both looked highly comical. But there was another blatant truth that was evident in the picture – we looked happy. It was the last time we had visited the fair. It was also the day when we had come closest into confessing what is now just a lie.

'There's something that's been bugging me for a long time,

you know,' he said.

'What is it?'

'Well, I don't know. You probably know it yourself.'

'What is it? I don't get it.'

'I know it's wrong. I probably shouldn't. But it's not mine to control anymore.'

'You are making no sense, do you know that?'

'I love you,' he mumbled indistinctly.

'What?' I asked, my heart almost skipping a beat.

'Nothing. Forget it. Let's get some pretzels.'

I put the picture back in my wallet and wiped the windshield that had turned slightly murky. I stepped out of the car and walked towards the cafe. Our usual seat, near the almost broken jukebox was empty. I sat down, my heart beating fast at the thought of him arriving any moment. 'Things could've been so different,' I thought.

After about a long fifteen minutes or so, I saw him enter through the glass door. He didn't change at all – the same tall and lean figure, that slight stubble on his chin, the rimless spectacles and those deep brown eyes behind them. I smiled at him. He smiled back as he walked towards me.

'You've come,' he said, his eyes brightening up.

'Of course.'

'You still look the same.'

'And so do you.'

He took the chair opposite to me. 'I'm so glad you could make it. I'd a strange feeling that you wouldn't come.'

'You're wrong. But I've got to head home soon. Loads of work.' I laughed nervously.

He didn't question me about my urgent work on a weekend.

He must have understood that I was lying.

'So, big day tomorrow, huh?' I tried to start a conversation.

'Pretty nervous, if you ask me. Too many responsibilities. A hundred more expectations.'

'And a thousand more promises to keep.'

He looked at me and gave out an uncertain sigh. 'Everything's happening so fast. I feel so nervous. I feel like I can't do this alone.'

'But you're not alone. She is with you,' I said, looking at him. 'She will be there. You're doing this with her, okay? Trust me, you'll be fine. You will be happy.'

'Won't you be there?'

'As a friend, I will. Always.'

'You know how I've – well, you know.'

I waited for him to finish his sentence. I saw the unspoken words trail off.

'It's okay. You don't have to.'

We stayed silent for a long time, gazing at nothing. I could sense how distant we had become and the realization slowly dawned upon me that things would never be the same again. For a moment, I had this burning desire to confront him, to know the truth. But sometimes, truth remains better unspoken and undisturbed. Knowing it to be the better option, I let that desire fade away.

'I should be going now,' I said, breaking the silence.

'But...'

'I have to. Congratulations again. I am very happy for both of you.'

'You should know that...' he hesitated for a moment, 'well, you should know that no one can ever replace you. Thank you for everything.'

Those words almost made me betray myself as I sensed my eyes turning blurry. I suppressed the sudden anguish blazing inside me with a smile.

'Good luck for your future,' I said, getting up.

'I would like it if you can make it tomo...'

'You know I can't.'

'I know.'

He walked me to my car and kissed me on my forehead before I got in. I kissed him on his left cheek. Some things never change.

I looked at him from the side view mirror, long enough to imprint his image in my memory. We both knew what we really shared. It was the greatest truth in our lives. But life is never that simple. Small truths must always give way for the greater truths. For in front of these greater truths, the smaller ones metamorphose into lies. And in this short and fleeting thing called Life, we can rarely indulge in these insignificant lies, no matter how important they may be.

Debakanya Haldar
(Guest Author)

3

Shackles of the Night Sky

The night was still young and brutality was at its peak. The cry of another Tutsi woman was striking the heart of Rwanda with its shrill pitch. Their greater wealth of once-upon-a-time was back in their lives to haunt them and humanity was moving past like a dead man walking. Anger was overflowing in the streets every day and also at the nights from the genitals of the Hutu men. We were inside our little thatched house made of clay.

'Oh Jesus!' I said turning towards Abel as the unrest continued outside, 'I fail to imagine we're two sets of people who raised cattle together and look at us now.'

'It's Aaron, you know?' Abel said, tucking his once yellow shirt into his long skirt, wrapped around his waist.

I always knew Aaron was a cruel man. However, he was regarded as the leader of our clan, the Hutus. Everyone feared him, for his command, influence and powerful men, and that's what made him the spearhead. A year back when things weren't as dreadful between the Hutus and the Tutsis, Aaron had killed hundreds of Hutu men and raped their women who were also from our clan, those who had objected to his actions and didn't do as he had ordered. 'My command is simple,' he would say, 'Men, bring out your inner beasts and take ten Tutsi women a day and kill their husbands, fathers and sons. I want to finish the Tutsis off. Women, pray that your husbands should mark my words lest

I and my men will get you!' People hated Aaron but no one dared to speak a word against him.

'Now what's with that inhuman bastard?' I asked.

'Hush, Nallely, Jesus Christ! We're under the watch list of our fellow Hutus! I can't see you get used by him or anybody else! We have to show support at the very least. Aaron just cautioned me to use my shaft proper or else...' Abel said while he made a clicking noise with his blue beaded necklace. I was taken aback by his remark.

'You'll use your shaft proper, meaning cut off the bellies of the neighborhood Tutsi women and pull out their unborn children! Again?'

'Nallely, oh Nallely! People have gone mad! They just won't let the lesser black Tutsis live in the world. None of them!'

'And you'll support the cause, Abel?'

'At least I'll show that I do. It seems the most right thing to do now – to save our lives, our baby. Had the Europeans not come in the past and made racial discriminations between the Tutsis' light and our dark skin colours, Nallely. For years, this superiority had given them the leadership positions even though they contributed a rather small fraction of the total population. For so many years. This was ought to happen! Had the Tutsis not misused their power, had they not shot our President's plane in the city of Kigali, they could've been a lot better off. The plane was shot down, they killed our President...he was a good man and now I don't think there is any escape from this. Sometimes I feel that all this is right.'

'How can it be right when each day thousands of men are being killed, women killed worse and children worst? How? This is a genocide!'

'I'd really thought after having those two Tutsi sisters, Yadira and Abassi, killing Abassi and handing her husband over to Aaron, and setting their house on fire thereafter...I thought I could prove something. I was utterly wrong. Aaron isn't happy that Yadira could flee with Abassi's son. He wants destruction. I've heard Abassi's husband has been killed near Nyarubuye Church. People say he had to pay for expensive bullets, before he died, for a quicker death! His body was thrown into the river. Yet, this isn't enough.'

Abassi was, by birth, from the Tutsi clan, the lesser black Africans from the northern parts. She lived as our neighbour for many years with her husband, her son of two months and Yadira, her sister. How I wish the family wasn't a victim to this...to the Hutus, to Abel.

Abassi was pretty and so was Yadira. The three of us made good company in the evenings for coffee. Abassi was the most composed woman I'd met. Her floor-length skirt would shine like a golden robe from the light of the lamp at the corner. Her shoulder would be draped with a sash. She and her husband made a lovely couple. On some evenings, I would urge Abassi to let their son stay with us. What fun we had, and then he would sleep in my arms. Contempt, anger and fear filled my eyes as I recalled what Abel was forced to do to their family.

I realised tear drops forming at the corner of my eyes and I quickly wiped them off. Abel put an arm around me.

'Thousands! Abel, thousands are dead already, or even more,' I said slowly, 'some of their remains are left to be eaten by rats and dogs! Cruel!' I turned towards Abel and continued, 'You've killed Abassi. We don't know where Yadira is. It's been months, died perhaps, of shame!'

'And you think that's enough? Women are getting raped ten times a day. I'm afraid, Aaron isn't that pleased with me. Though he spares me because you're not keeping well most of the time.'

'Let him not be pleased then. I can't let another soul die for my sake. Let him take out my unborn!'

'Heaven's sake, Nallely!'

'Heaven's? Do you hope to be there any day after all that's going on?'

'Nallely, try to understand, dear. Hell is anyway waiting down there. There can be nothing better. The clergy in our Church has also colluded with Aaron. And I am going to do it. Again.'

Abel left...leaving the door open. I took off the two ribbons. That's how Abassi had taught me to tie my hair in a bun on a lazy summer afternoon; the ribbons passed across the forehead, crossing above the ear. The beads from the bun dropped on the floor and so did the comb that was clutched in my hair. I felt I could see Abassi looking at me from a corner...she seemed to have a lot of questions which I didn't know how to answer. I sat down on the bed. My hands shivered as I caressed my unborn child. It shouldn't be a girl, I thought, who will never have any say against rapes, no say if her husband uses another woman, no say whatsoever. It shouldn't be a boy, I thought again, and become like the blood thirsty men, perhaps like my husband. Probably, I kept thinking, it was better unborn in the ominous land of Rwanda. As I cried, I could see Abassi and her husband, like shadows in a hazy half-lit world. I thought they would laugh at my misery, abuse me for what Abel did to them. I cried and cried. I didn't know how to stop Abel, he was the most loving husband...that's what I always knew. I wished he would cry, shout, scream, he was also in so much pain for what he was forced to do.

It was midnight. A light was showing up from the east window, a tinge of paler grey on the horizon. Abel was yet to return. A storm rose up. I stood up and walked a couple of steps forward to close the window when there was a sharp pain and I felt what seemed like a strong menstrual cramp. There was intense stretching, like a burning sensation. I walked back slowly to the bed. The storm calmed down and it began to rain. There wasn't a woman I could turn to for help. The entire neighborhood almost, except a few women from my clan, was being raped...one of them was probably being used by Abel, I thought. I closed my eyes and clutched a pillow. I could feel my forehead sweating profusely when I heard Abel calling out, 'Nallely! Nallely...'

✦

The first rays of the sun broke open the shackles of the night sky. I had seen a dream which had Abassi, her husband, their son, Yadira, and Abel and our child...it seemed perfect, everyone was there and happy. I woke up and felt a shiver run down my spine as I realised the sweet but vague might-have-been dream. I turned to look at my new born daughter, sleeping soundly beside me.

'Good morning, Nallely.' It was Abel. I clenched my jaw muscles. Fear occupied my mind.

'Abel! Don't come any nearer! You did it again? Oh Jesus, spare my child for his sins,' I clutched the pillow and looked away.

'No no Nallely...I didn't touch a soul. I didn't. Aaron gave me a woman and went away. Good God had always been with me and I found a hiding place for her. She'll be safe by His grace.'

'You didn't even touch the woman? What about the women who stand by the rapists as spectators? Why would they let this happen?'

'I met Aaron and he took me inside a dark and shallow hut near our Church. The women were all there. But Aaron had some work, I don't know what, but he was about to leave. I knew I couldn't do it again. No matter what, I knew I had to get out of that place without harming anyone this time and I had to be quick. I observed him carefully as he walked to the door. I knew that time was running out but suppressed the urge to check my watch. I took a deep breath and started counting in reverse under my breath. 'Ten, nine, eight, seven...' As soon as he left the wind started blowing hard and then the rain poured down like some unfamiliar blessing. The women, all of them, left the spot leaving the two of us behind.'

A tear appeared at the corner of his eyes that shone like a diamond on his black skin. I kept staring at him.

'When I was about to leave for home,' he continued, 'the woman Aaron gave me called me by my name. Her voice sounded so familiar and I was really taken aback when I found she was none other than Yadira.' I couldn't repress a mild shiver and covered my mouth with my hands.

'Yadira! So she's alive? Did you ask her about Abassi's son?'

I stood up. I took our daughter to my chest as tightly as I could. With my eyes firmly shut I let my tears run down my face. God, keep them safe, please God, I kept murmuring, my eyes still closed. A sharp cry stirred me. I opened my eyes. There was a child in Abel's hands.

'This is him, Nallely. Yadira gave me this...a chance to clear my sins. After they all left I urged Yadira to run away. She told me Abassi's child would eventually die if he was to stay with her. I brought Abassi's baby boy here with me.'

I felt a gentle flurry of air across my face. The infant clutched Abel's shirt with his tiny fingers strongly, like he would to his father. I could feel happiness from my stomach. Abel sat down beside me and carefully made him lie down on the bed.

'Nallely? Can we? Can we have him? Can he not grow up with our princess,' he said softly, smoothing the windblown strands of hair from my face.

The tenderness in his voice was overwhelming. This was the Abel I had longed to see, I thought. I couldn't hold back the joy of having him back. 'Oh yes! Oh yes! Abel, we'll have him too! Bring him here. Come to Mama!'

I inclined my head on Abel's chest, feeling his warmth and the strength of his arms around me. I looked out of the window. It was a bright morning and the sun was just beyond the trees that lined our house. We sat locked together for a moment, swaying slightly in the wind that entered through the window, welcoming the newly found happiness in our family. I carefully took the baby boy in my arms. I felt I saw Abassi and her husband from the corner again...looking at their child and probably, blessing him and all of us.

'Abel! He is our child. God has shown mercy upon us this time, I feel he will grow up to look like me.' Abel drew back a bit, smiling down at me.

The morning freshness was again interrupted by another shrill voice but for us it was morning after many dark nights. It was a beautiful day, with the burgeoning greenery of the trees coming alive through the little window...the greenery that rimmed the endless sky.

4

The Crazed Lover

That was the eventful day on which we'd received our admission letters from the Indian Institute of Management, Lucknow.

'Hi Naina,' said a striking voice over the phone, 'Nihant here, congratulations!'

'To you too, Nihant! I'm so excited, you know! This is my first convert of the season, the best that I can get. Same for you as well?'

'Absolutely, my interview for admissions, you wouldn't believe, went for as long as ninety minutes, seemed it wouldn't end. I wasn't very sure how it went. I was nervous since morning, you know, until now that the e-mail has finally come! Man, my room is in a clutter. I couldn't concentrate on anything.'

'Ah, I know, I've been going through the same spin of emotions all day. It feels strange, kind of bizarre, to have met on Facebook and talk over the phone without meeting. I've always thought you look like a kid in you profile picture, don't mind, but I'm taken aback by your voice, sounds much mature. So how have you been?'

'Good so far! Awesome now. And don't call me a kid, li'l girl!'

'It's going to be such a thrill the day we all meet in the campus. We'll all keep guessing each other.'

'In this world of social media, guessing? Unlikely! But it is going to be delightful! What are your plans till then? I'm going on a couple of treks.'

'I'll read as much as I can...I've heard once you're inside the campus, it becomes difficult to do your readings.'

'What do you read?'

'Oh, I love reading classics.'

'Ah, Jane Austen?'

'And Charlotte Bronte, Leo Tolstoy, Charles Dickens, his *A Tale of Two Cities* most noteworthy, and lately, Diana Gabaldon.'

'So who's your favourite? Darcy? Or Heathcliff?'

'Ha...ha, I can't really believe we're having this discussion in real. I loved Darcy as a teenage girl. He seemed like a dream. Now I feel there's nothing special about him that should make him my favourite. Heathcliff is more appealing, with his unusual ways of love. But one character I'm really, really into is Sydney Carton. His sacrifice!'

'From Charles Dicken's? I haven't yet read *A Tale of Two Cities*. I must; if it's your favourite it must be worth a read. It really seems you'd love to go to England some day? Wouldn't you?'

'And do what?'

'Have tea, and dance in the balls?'

'I'd like to go to Ireland, rather.'

'Ireland! That's so odd. I dream of being there ever since...'

'Yes, ever since I've watched *P. S. I Love You*.'

'You've got me there, Naina!' he said and we kept laughing for some time. I could feel an instant connection with Nihant the moment we started conversing over the phone. For the next couple of weeks we spoke every second day, discussing the rain and thunderstorm, lilies, crocus-like pink flowers that sprang up on the hillsides.

Another week passed. It was my first day in Lucknow and the campus was stunning. Spread over a hundred and eighty five acres, I felt it was an ideal setting conducive to learning. I was enthralled by its setting in the serene and verdant vicinity. The exquisite design began with a huge sculpture of Arjuna on the chariot with his mentor, Krishna...a still from the Mahabharata. And then we entered a world of salient red bricks, lined up to form medieval Indian structures. The intricate planning ensured that nature is maintained at its splendid best in a campus brimming with articulately designed buildings, well-manicured lawns and stands of large trees on a beautiful site. The trees were well maintained, but at night, they looked quite creepy. They moved front, back and sideways...dancing with the air in the darkness. There were a number of food joints – the Not Just Tea stall dazzled in the yellow light...the Gossip n Bite in the white...the Nescafe shop...the Juice Corner...and the beautifully lit Annapoorna Mess. All the festivity, the glamour, the light, the food, the happy faces of the otherwise serious, intellectual or always-in-a-hurry crowd of students didn't take me long to fall in love with the place.

I met a population of diverse background from lawyers to musicians to cricketers and pharmacists. It was the month of June and monsoons had just begun to settle down. I walked up the steps to the beautifully festooned Samanjasya Hall.

I was lost in the experience I was going through when suddenly I remembered Nihant. He wasn't there. Was he late? Did he miss his flight? I recalled we hadn't spoken for a week almost. After those warm, late night conversations for days, there was a snap in the attachment that had begun, a break that was so abrupt. I quickly dialled his number to call him. It was getting dark.

'Nihant? Where are you? Come to the mess if you're in the campus.'

'Naina. I'm not joining IIM Lucknow,' came the reply. There was an uninterrupted silence for some time.

'What nonsense, Nihant? Nihant, are you unwell?'

'I'll tell you all that later. I'm not joining IIM Lucknow, I'd have loved to, you know.'

'Yes, I know. We did discuss all that.'

'I'm joining some other college, maybe XLRI or FMS. They are great options! Take care, Naina!' he said and the line got disconnected.

He was rude. I was angry, but more than anything else I could feel severe convolutions inside my heart. Everything turned hazy. My heart was beating fast...it was so loud that I could almost hear it. Suddenly, I felt a pat on my shoulders. I turned around.

'Naina! It's Nihant!'

Light was glistening throughout the place in festivity for the new batch of students and I could see Nihant, his eyes fixed on mine. I was meeting him for the first time. We were in an open-air lawn, with lots of trees complementing the velvet-veiled tables and chairs. I smiled at him, his eyes brimful of innocence, and a handsome face that wore a grin, ear to ear. He was smiling comfortingly as we walked towards a bench nearby past the trees, the Greek paintings, the sculptures and the pillars. The trees were still. Not a single leaf moved. The grass was silent and the music stopped playing, the boys and girls around, dressed in business formals disappeared, the eating joints faded away, it was only the two of us under the starry sky. I walked to him in a blue polka dot dress tied in the front. It was like magic. We sat down on a bench nearby. I gave him an impulsive and tight hug.

'You're smiling so much and it absolutely suits you,' he said, 'it's always so nice to see a pleasant smile as this one you're wearing.'

'And you don't look anything like your profile picture on

Facebook! So we haven't spoken for almost a week now. You've been preparing for this prank? Atrocious!'

'And how much I'd enjoyed those few seconds.'

'You're as cunning as serpents.'

'I think you're cute! As cute as buttons?'

'I at times wonder what would've happened if we were in the same group discussion for IIM L admission process.'

'Would we fight?'

'Badly,' I said.

'Like cats. Would've bought the other an ice cream later, for sure. Ice creams help bring friends together. Always.'

'Always! That's my favourite word in the English language, you know. I love this word. It's like a promise.'

'Well Naina, on this first meeting, you'll have to give me a chance of asking you anything, and I mean anything. That one question that I want to ask you at the onset of this beautiful evening, under the prettiest sky so bedecked with the stars. And promise to answer it honestly, no lies, promise.' I agreed. He looked at me and thinking briefly said, 'Do you think we're soulmates?'

'Define soulmates.'

'The one person you have an immediate connection with, the very moment you meet. The one you can be yourself with, confidently. What do you think is a soulmate?'

'I don't believe in soulmates,' I said. It was getting uncomfortable. 'We're friends, right? Have you watched a movie recently?' I asked.

'Wait, do not change the topic. Do you have an answer for me? Otherwise Naina, I have to grieve the loss of you as a lover before I can appreciate the gain of you as a dear friend. I couldn't speak to you for the last one week, I was confused about us. I'm sure about my feelings now that I stand before you. I know this is abrupt on the very first meeting, but I truly feel as if we've known each other for ages. That's the kind of connection I've had with you.' I turned to look at him. His face turned dull and disappointed.

'Nihant, I've barely known you.'

'How long, Naina, will it take for you to know me?'

'I'll let you know.'

As I saw the seasons changing, my love for the campus was intensified and it gradually started to feel like home. From the beautiful autumn hues to the foggy cold nights of the winter I enjoyed it all.

The scenic beauty of the campus was at par with the academic pressure. Sleepless nights had already begun for us. Campus life was more synonymous to strong coffee and chicken rolls, the management jargons and the classes that got drowsier than ever. Nihant was in a different section and we seldom met after that awkward first meeting.

Sections in IIM Lucknow is a very significant element of campus life. Section A for me was like family. I made some great friends here. I met fashion designers, musicians, writers and some amazing people. Whenever there would be a birthday, it used to be the sixty students from the same section who would order the cakes, present unkind birthday bumps and throw eggs, ketchups, toothpaste and almost anything in sight at the poor chap. And gradually, each one of us developed a sense of difference, a feeling of contrast with folks who belonged to a different section.

At times, I wanted to speak to Nihant about how the sky changed colour in the most magical of all places I've been. I often questioned such cravings...why out of all people, Nihant?

And then I would quickly dismiss the short-lived thoughts. Just like me, he had formed a world of his own. Section C seemed absolutely close to him...be it inside classrooms or outside...in the mess, swimming pool, badminton court. I learnt he was engaged to someone his family knew. Bit by bit, in between the drowsy classes combined with scores of inter-college competitions and placement preparations, Nihant disappeared from my area of interest.

Academic pressure kept building up with every passing day. Over the months, we were gradually getting adapted to the uncanny demands of projects and exams during odd times of the day and sleep had become a rare commodity. We had quizzes to study for and assignments to work on even on our birthdays. I celebrate my birthday on 21st November, and the day had arrived with only a week left for the term papers. I was too worked up with my books to go outside and celebrate. As the last hint of orange dropped beyond the academic building, I sat down at my table in a pensive state of mind. I looked up and the ceiling stared back. I remembered Nihant, unexpectedly. I wished if he would have celebrated with me, done something special, perhaps called or texted me. The room was closed. The walls felt like coming closer with every moment of thinking how life would've been had Nihant been the same old Nihant I had known. Are we soulmates, why am I thinking about him out of all the people I know on this day, I wondered. Just then my phone began to ring. It was Nihant.

'Yes, tell me,' I answered.

'I wish you a happy birthday, Naina. How's life?'

'Amazing! I'm having so much fun here! Can't you see I'm inside my hostel on my birthday? Where are you?'

'You don't sound as if you're happy? Naina? What's wrong?'

I thought I would say – You! Nihant! I miss you here! I don't get the link we had with anyone in campus. You've left me alone. You've made new friends, new connections. And here I am. I crave for energy, hope, direction. 'Nothing's wrong. I've got a quiz tomorrow morning. Financial Management Quiz 2.' The phone call felt particularly strange. I started sensing a rush of vacuum inside my heart, like never before.

For the next few days the words kept coming back to my mind – Do you think we're soulmates? My feelings for Nihant were going through a transformation, I could understand the change, and I could do nothing to keep them anchored. On some days I wanted to shout out, 'Nihant, I love you! On Thursdays, when Section C has the 12:30 p.m. simulation class inside the Computer Centre, I stand right near the lounge to see you. I stand there for half an hour, missing my lectures, worrying myself to sick that I wouldn't see you. I was wrong, I walked away! But since then you've been so indifferent too. The smile you pass at me when we cross each other's paths on our way to our classrooms, they hurt me! A mere smile is not what I expect from you, Nihant.' I would gulp my words in silence, rush to a washroom and cry myself to peace.

✦

Days, weeks and months passed. It was spring. We had a week, one lecture and four exams remaining before campus life would come to an end. One afternoon, sitting in the library, I came across IIM Pulse, the quarterly magazine. It was an old volume, almost a year old. The catchy cover page held my attention. I flipped through the pages till I reached the end of it. The last page had a poem:

To the Days
I'm walking down the patched road,
In the middle of the way to Medusa.
Deep down in torn pockets,
I firmly curl my thumb
I hum our old tunes; never mind the bard, his couplets.
People come and go, some stop and cough.
Some cough and stop, few wait for the dust to clear.
There's a feline voice, whispering into my ear,
She speaks of the place where all is forgiven
And forgotten, maybe.
She speaks equal parts, water and wind.
She knows I run, from the world, from myself
She tells me she knows where to hide –
Deep in the cove by the clamouring sea,
Where the Sun's rays gratify idle, stony feet.
I see your countenance in the crushing crowd,
You in a blue polka dot dress, tied in the front, with a smile.
Our eyes meet for a while but we walk away
With lively steps towards adamant voices.
Hark! I hear the clinking of a far-away bell.
Did you hear it as well?
I have faith, our paths may cross again
If you read this, know I'm yours, Always...
Till then, go work your shadowy ways!
Have a great birthday, Naina

Written by Nihant Sharma
First Year, Section C

In the evening, I was sitting inside the Operations Management class, the last lecture that would end our MBA journey. Nihant's poem left me astounded. The chalk hit my nose. The precision with which silence was torn open into a roar of laughter struck my ears like a sharp pin of embarrassment. That was the professor's forte, hitting with the chalk whenever he saw a student unmindful in his class. The professor's slide on the projector read, "You never get a second chance...to make a first impression." I was startled by the irony of the moment. I recalled my first encounter with Nihant. I wanted to talk to him and realised I'd forgotten my phone on my bed before leaving for the class.

I excused myself from the class and was on my way to speak to him. I understood the perils of it; he might have forgotten about the poem he wrote a year back, he is engaged to someone dear to him and calling him would seem absolutely lame. I heard a muffled howl of nervousness from behind me, then a hysterical anxiety from the reverse direction. It was getting dark fast, and I pushed my way through the shorter road to the hostel, through the bushes and the grass as quickly as was possible. I was indeed hopeful. I ran as fast as I could. It was nearly full dark by then; the bright moonlight had flooded the road. At times it felt as if the shadows of the trees were stalking me.

I reached my room. My phone was exactly where I had expected. I typed on it, 'What does it mean to be an adult? What does it mean to be well and truly on your own? What does it mean to lose people? What does it mean...the word destiny? How are you?'

A message flashed on the screen after sometime. 'Why are your words disconnected? I'm getting married in another month. I do not know if I want his. Just going with the flow, pre-decided by parents. Do you think you know me enough now? Nihant.'

The words filled my eyes with tears and I quickly wiped them off. 'Congratulations! Have a great life ahead,' I texted back.

✦

College life had come to an end. After being grilled trimester after trimester for quizzes, submissions and exams I'd never imagined I would miss IIM Lucknow. I started working for Deloitte in Mumbai. I was getting used to late night meetings, early morning flights and then the local train rush. The transition from college to corporate life was very rapid and intense, with no preparation lesson or brochures. The only place I liked inside the office building was the sea-facing cafeteria. I enjoyed watching the waves for half an hour every evening before leaving for the day. This was where I would think about myself, wonder about my purpose, and decide upon resolutions. Sometimes Nihant would cross my mind, but that would be for a short while. A very short while.

On a rainy evening, facing the sea, sitting on a wooden bench inside the cafeteria and looking at nothingness I was enjoying the fresh bout of breeze.

'Hey Naina,' I thought I heard Nihant. I looked up. I saw Nihant's eyes smiling at mine. 'Naina! How're you?'

'Nihant! You're here? In Mumbai?'

'The company has sent some of us for a day long training in Mumbai...so I happen to be here. My office is on the third floor.'

'How's work?'

'However the work is, mortals like us end up liking whatever we do.'

'Nihant, you're here...a pleasant surprise! I don't know what to say.'

'I realize you're much better with me over the phone than in the real world. We barely spoke in campus! And here you are. Seeing me after months. Still don't know what to say.'

'How's she?' I said after a short snap in the conversation.

'Who she?'

'Your wife, silly! How's married life?'

'Come on Naina. Do I come across that old to you that I've started looking like I'm married?'

'What nonsense, Nihant. I remember you'd told me about your marriage.'

'Yet, you do not remember what I'd asked you in the end of my message. This is the problem with girls. You people concentrate on insignificant details which kills everything.'

'We're meeting after very long. Do you wish to fight?' Nihant sat down, facing me.

'I'm asking for one last time. Naina, do you know me enough to love me?'

'Your jokes are pathetic!'

'I'm not married. I cannot marry anyone else. Naina, I love you. I tried to be honest in what had transpired in those few heady weeks when we spoke almost every day before joining college. You showed me the door. And your reasons being you do not know me enough. It was always awkward to speak to you after that. I'd tried on your birthday. I wanted to speak about my feelings to you again. I feared your judgements about me would change for the worse. And then I thought I would write down my feelings. You read that poem? I thought you never did, and even if you'd read it you chose to ignore it, since you never asked me. That made my assumption all the more clear that you're not into me. I did recognize the inevitability that we should drift apart on separate ways. I drifted myself away because I wanted to be in my peace, far from you. I tried to find love in someone else. In two years, I realized that was far-fetched, for there's only misery away from you. And now I regret all that. I should've bottled up courage and not hide myself inside my cocoon shell and made sure that you know me enough.'

'That was a beautiful birthday gift, Nihant. Thank you so much!'

'And that's all you've got for me? I'll always love you. Always. Like a promise.'

'Why? Nihant? Don't say this please. It's like we're never on the same page. My parents have seen a guy for me. Don't say this! I'm engaged.'

'I can't help it, how can I?' he continued, 'you're the proverbial forbidden apple and at the same time, panacea to my human condition. And if I were to be thrown out of God's garden, then so be it. All this while I kept telling myself, you're yet another girl. But you were not, you are not. And finally, meeting today, after months, floored me. The heart is hopeful again. I sound so sappy, you know. But that's how the entreaties of the heart are. If I were to have a better half, I can't imagine anyone but you fulfilling the part. In the past two years, my heart was in agony. My mind schemed that it should let it go on as long as it would. But my heart foresaw that time was running out. And it has run out. Finally. And you are the flawless angel in my eyes. You'll always be. But I'm alone, alone as alone can be. Call me a crazed lover twenty years from now.'

'You'll be a dear friend always.'

'It will break my heart to the tiniest pieces, so tiny that it can't be stitched together. Go away, you deserve better.'

'Let's go home, Nihant. Do get some sleep. You're not well.'

'Why? When I'm most awake? When liquid courage courses through my veins? I can keep talking all night and day, if you would permit. But I've crossed all boundaries.'

'You're a great guy. You'll get a great girl! You'll get a princess.'

'Why can't you be that great girl?' he kept his eyes fixed on mine and after a brief moment of disturbing silence, he continued, 'who needs a princess? Nothing changes. I don't deserve your kindness.'

'I'm not being kind.'

'No, you're being what you are. And I can't love you enough for that.'

'I'm sorry. You've been worse than you were before you'd met me. I'm the reason for your unhappiness and misfortune.'

'Don't be sorry. I'm happy now. I can't stay sad or happy enough for long. Can you? I dread I'll be sad again. No escape. Really. I'll continue to hope. For as long it takes. Till I see the rituals done and you betrothed to someone else. But I can never forget you. Don't take away the hope. Let it die in its own death in due time. Let me curl up in my misery.'

'I'm sorry, Nihant.'

'Please don't be sorry, Naina. It'll be alright. It'll run its usual course and heal before long. Let's leave now, on our own separate ways and promise each other never to meet again.' He stood up and said, 'I wish you'd find happiness in your life. All the while I had been thinking about us. Even if you felt an iota of what I did for you it would have sufficed. I never had been sure till today that it was all in my head. Let me be alone and in my peace. Seeing you is a constant reminder of what might have been.'

'Where are you going, Nihant?'

'To a place of my own. Hope you understand and allow me not to communicate with you for however long it takes for this change to sink in.' He quietly stood up and walked outside the cafeteria.

I kept staring at him as he slowly paced outside the door. He lowered his head as he walked out of my sight. I could not move. His words recurrently played inside my mind. I felt a sudden rush of emotions. I wasn't sure if I was still in love with him. But I was in love, every starry night, windy noon and clear mornings, for the past two years, most of it.

I told myself,

'Hope is never lost
Stays as long as the flower lives
Tears make it grow strong
The tiny seed forever believes
To start fresh – a journey, happy and long.
Without you it may seem dull
Dark and empty like the overcast dawn.
And that's but momentary
Since life knows exactly how to move on.'

The wind shifted and swept the cloud away. The curtains that covered the huge windows swayed erratically as the wind swept past the tall trees outside and moaned in all the leaves and branches – whosh...whoosh...whhooosshhh. I looked outside at the dusty, wind-drenched road. I walked out of the cafeteria, away from the most crazed lover I've known, towards home.

5

A Handful of Soil

Sitting on the string bed under the guava tree, whose leaves were just beginning to turn yellow, my grandmother was ruminating deeply over something. She rested her chin on her knees and gazed across the garden. She was smiling on her own – as if coloured slides were slipping across the projector of the memory. She was very old, with white hair, wearing a white sari with a maroon border.

'Dida, what happened, you're sitting here all by yourself?'

She slowly turned towards me, the sun shining on both her wrinkles. Her skin had creased considerably towards the edges of her eyes, though she carried her age-lines gracefully.

'I was thinking about the question you asked me this morning,' she said. Her broken voice suggested that she had gone back in time.

'Ah that one about defining success in your own words? So did you come up with your answer – what success means to you? It'll be helpful for my research paper.'

'Tuli, I've been thinking about it since then. And yes, I think I know what success means to me – it is when you look back at your life and the memories make you smile. That's what success is to me.'

Her reply made my heart melt. I moved closer to Dida and said, 'What makes you say this? What makes you smile?'

I noticed the right corner of the lips slightly tilt upwards as she smiled and recalled, 'When I was very small, we lived in Bangladesh. My father was a renowned advocate and we lived in a very big house. But nothing then was ours or mine. We lived together with the poorest and the richest. We had a radio which people across the lanes nearby would come to listen...listen to the morning bhajans.'

'What about privacy? Early morning, so many people, did it not cause disturbance?'

'Back then, people were not as busy as now. We used to live like extended families. And then we had Kanai Da, our cook. He made amazing *Alu Posto, Kach Kolar Kofta* and *Muitha of Chitol Maach.* Whenever he cooked *Moong Daal* with *Maacher Maatha* I would be loaded with boundless joy. But that didn't mean we would have the food all by ourselves. It would be a mini feast in our house with all the neighbours coming in.'

'Was Kanai Da such a good cook? Had he been here I would have asked him to make all my favorite dishes.'

'Oh yes, Kanai Da was a connoisseur cook. He could pass on mouth-watering magic to any mundane vegetable...any.'

'So Moong Daal – your favorite – was it?'

'I loved it, yes, but my favorite dish by Kanai Da was *Gathi* or *Arbi* as we call it now.'

'Arbi! What's so special about that? It's a pretty tasteless thing. I'm sure he cooked more succulent stuff.'

'But Kanai Da had magic at the tip of his fingers. I enjoyed the entire process of cooking Arbi – the way he would do. He peeled the vegetables – the entire pieces with utmost tenderness and care – gliding the knife around every contour – as if he was caressing it. Then gradually, one by one he would fry them in clarified butter till they turned yellowish – slightly golden. He waited for the pieces to get supple. He then added spices and herbs to flavor them. And yes, he made his own spices – back then we had no ready-made sachets of masala.'

'I get it. It's seeing the whole cooking experience that made Arbi your favorite dish!'

'And Kanai Da did it so well. He was not just a cook, I'd say he was an artist – who never parted with his recipes like any good cook. I was very fond of him. I enjoyed visiting the marketplace with Kanai Da.'

'Was the marketplace different in those days?'

'Oh yes, a lot. There was so much secrecy in business. The merchants announced their prices clandestinely with fingers since lips could be read.'

'Even fingers can be seen!'

'So they had towels to cover their hands and convey the prices only to the prospective customers. I don't remember the signs too well – it was something like a clasp of two fingers would mean two rupees and likewise.'

'This was amazing. I've never heard or read about this anywhere earlier.'

'Yes and gradually this practice became extinct and people forgot about it. I remember once when my mother fell ill and I was around six years old, Kanai Da took every responsibility on himself that my mother had. We had no electricity back then. We cooled my mother by pouring sand and then we sprinkled water on the thick layer of it thrice a day.'

She put both her hands together in front of her feet as she sat cross-legged on the bed and with childlike glee she was shaking one of her legs and continued, 'When my parents were out, I sometimes insisted Kanai Da to bathe me. He would bathe and dress me with utmost tenderness. What I loved the most then was his typical way of shielding me against everyone, including my parents. He did some strange things too. We had this huge peepul tree behind our house. It would be very cool in the evenings to sit beneath it. The heart shaped leaves would swing around in the air cooling the air down through its branches. Oh and did I ever tell you, my father planted lots of trees in our garden – our garden was my favorite spot in the house and I really enjoyed sitting there, doing nothing, touching the leaves and watching them grow. So once a week, I saw Kanai Da would keep a saucer of milk under the shade of the tree and in some time a cobra – a long thin snake – would glide to the saucer and gradually empty the container.'

'Was he always this good? Did you make him angry ever or did he scold you at times?'

'Oh yes he did. He managed to scare me a lot when he said I should not stay in the garden, beneath the trees after it got dark – he said silly things like the spirits come and sit on the trees – and little as I was, I believed his words strongly. He said other things like snapping twice with my fingers whenever I felt like yawning would make me stronger. He had a wrestler's arms. Most children would draw away from him in fright – his gigantic size and quivering lips were the most impenetrable. He had thick, curly hair. He would get angry when I wouldn't listen to him – he was a very strict disciplinarian. His face looked like the menacing thundercloud when he got angry. I managed to infuriate him really hard when I tiptoed into the kitchen with dirty shoes – he was so angry – I still remember, though he never beat me up, he scolded. But when he smiled with delight it was as if the sun had just emerged, highlighting his sharp facial features with a great dazzle.'

'So he came here with you to India. Or did he stay back there?'

'That's still a mystery. We left Bangladesh in1946 during the Noakhali riots and we lost track of Kanai Da. We tried a lot to look for him. It was on the Lakshmi Puja day – I think somewhere in October. I was ten years old. I remember there was so much upheaval since morning – people screaming, shouting, crying. My father, being a respectable advocate, was assured security and we reached India safely the next day. I only bear in mind lots and lots of people. I was so scared that I might get lost in the crowd. I clutched my father's hands as tightly as I could. I think we had lost Kanai Da in the crowd that day. He had nothing called a family – not that I knew or ever heard of. We were his family. He had no one else to spend the rest of his life with. And this is what has been bothering me so much all my life.'

'Did you see Kanai Da again after that?'

'No,' she blinked her eyes twice and said, 'never again. Later, I read somewhere that the Hindus were killed, women were raped, many were converted forcibly to Islam and in order to leave the country it required special permits. I prayed a lot for Kanai Da and all I could do was hope that he was safe.' She looked down at the grass that was turning October yellow. The trees were still and the birds were unusually silent. There was only the sound of crickets on the oak tree behind us. It seemed there could be a storm in the evening.

'Did you feel like going back to Bangladesh again?'

'Every moment of everyday. Often I wonder – how much of my childhood I've left behind there which has now become a foreign country. I left the place I grew up in a dash. I've never been able to visit Bangladesh after that or meet Kanai Da – find out what happened to him since sixty seven years.'

She took out an old transparent plastic bottle from under her sari. The yellow lid was cracked in parts. There was something reddish brown inside it. She squinted and looked closely at the jar. She carefully opened the lid, closed her eyes and took the smell. When she looked at me, I saw her eyes twinkle.

'You know what this is, Tuli? This is a handful of land I'd brought from my birth place on my way to India. I've valued this plastic jar more than anything else, all my rather long life. The sand, the pebbles, and little stones in it remind me how trouble-free yet beautiful my childhood had been with my mother, father and Kanai Da.'

'What if you would've got one opportunity to see Kanai Da? What would you say?'

She looked up. The sky was covered with clouds – the first ones approaching winter. It was slightly sultry. The left corner of her lips was shaking considerably as she recalled those days with Kanai Da and imagined to see him again.

'All my life,' she said, 'I've hoped that a day will come when I will go back to Bangladesh – or people from there would come to meet me and this would happen very frequently. And maybe then, I will be able to meet Kanai Da once again – ask him how he had been – if he had converted to Islam. And one thing I would surely request him to share – the secrets of his recipes.' She looked at me and continued, 'Tuli you'll have to do me a favor. Here, take this jar.'

I took the jar from her. Her hands were shaking considerably as she cautiously placed the old container in my hands. It was remarkable. I could almost see my grandmother running and playing and dancing on the soil as a little girl with Kanai Da – the soil that witnessed two groups of people fight – the soil that had seen a nation break into two.

'This is so beautiful. The pebbles look so fresh.' I opened the lid and took the smell and continued, 'The soil smells of your childhood – it smells of war – it smells of the land of the little imagination I had of Kanai Da.'

'This handful of soil holds lots of memories – so many of them I had captured inside this jar for years. Today, I want you to release the soil. Let both the lands meet – it's going to be amazing.'

I placed the lid on the bed and poured the soil out of the jar on the grass and watched my grandmother looking at it with mesmerized eyes. A yellow butterfly settled on the lid. I made a slight grab at it and it flew off and settled on a leaf of the guava tree. When the jar became empty the butterfly flew back towards us. This time it settled on the liberated soil on the grass.

6

The Empty Title

The taxi moved through the busy market of Nager Bazaar and Sharmila was memorizing the guitar notes from the chord book. She covered her ears with her fingers and continued muttering. The taxi took a sharp turn to the left and entered a narrow and dark lane. There were old buildings on either side. Soon the taxi came out of the lane and they were on the main road. As the sun slowly edged its way towards the horizon the notes and the chords blurred away. She was lost in her thoughts and the first time she had held a guitar when she was twelve came back to her mind....

'Ah! The fingers hurt!'

'Look at mine, Sharmila,' Lucy Ma'am had said, closely examining her fingers with furrowed brows, 'mine have become so hard with years of practice.'

'My fingers will become as hard as yours one day. Will they?'

'Yes it will. But you've got to work hard and practice every day. Ev-er-y-da-ay.'

Sharmila looked at her fingers. The tip had become hard over the years. She could not recall when her fingers had stopped paining. But she remembered the transition...initially the tips turned pink and then red...gradually became bluish, blackish... and now it was hard.

Sharmila was late. It showed fifteen minutes past 5 o'clock on her watch and her performance was about to begin in forty-five minutes. It was an important day for her and she was just minutes away from her debut show at Kalamandir. The sky looked blue and promising. The road was being continuously painted by combinations of cheerful hues made by the rays of the sun. It veiled her softly with the tender touch of its golden rays of hope, pointing to glorious fame in the world of music.

'*Bhaiya*,' she said, 'we need to make it quick please.'

The taxi driver was possibly in his forties and had few streaks of grey hair towards the temples on the forehead and near the ears. The skin under his eyes had a few small wrinkles that were fanning out prominently in the sun. He took out a dirty red piece of cloth from under his seat to rub the fare meter in the front. His grey shirt was partly tucked out of his trousers.

The taxi began to move past the shops, big and small. Sharmila looked back to see the greenery of trees along the sides of the street. The blue sky was a perfect combination to the lively green. The shops on the sides of the road ran away, behind the cab. The pleasant wind struck her face and she closed her eyes. When she opened them she noticed a white ambassador approaching closer. Eventually, it overtook their taxi, leaving them behind...stuck at a red signal.

It is truly impossible to travel on the roads of Kolkata these days, she thought. A large group of men and women were shouting from a distance, 'Stop it! Change it! *Bondho Korun*!' They could be heard more clearly as they approached. They walked in a straight line – shouting, screaming and protesting. They all looked angry and many of them were walking with large banners. A few of them carried painted flags in their hands. A tall, heavily built man who was walking in the front row was shouting a sentence in the microphone and every time he did that, the others shouted out in chorus. The broad street was almost overflowing with people and the busy market looked busier. Most of the women were in white saris and the men were wearing white kurta and trousers. The others who were not following the white dress code seemed to be just walking down for fun. The spectators talked among themselves and soon a group of people formed a discussion forum in front of the tea stall that stood on the footpath. A serious political discussion began. The driver showed keen interest in their conversation and tried to listen to the various opinions that they were putting forward. Sharmila noticed that he was particularly restless when he heard an old man raise his hand to stop others in the group in order to present his opinion. The noise of the protest was all around her, making her head spin and she felt dizzy. Her vision began to blur. She was lulled by the noise of the slowly moving crowd into an illusion of serene weightlessness.

There was a far-off banging noise that she rather dazedly identified as a car horn. 'Bhaiya.' she asked the taxi driver, 'how long will they take to clear the road?'

'Five, at most ten minutes, Didi,' the driver said, raising his brows censoriously, as though she had suggested that it would take longer. He looked irritated because of this interruption.

She began to worry a little. She looked at her watch, sticking a finger between the pages to mind her place. The minute hand on her watch was moving faster than ever. Her heart was beating fast.

'Didi, do you think it's good that the Nano project is taken off,' the driver asked. Sharmila was unmindful and stared at him blankly. 'What's gone is gone. They're not coming back. Who knows why all the protest and strike and everything else. What good does it bring to anyone?'

'I'm not sure if it does any good. But it has already made us quite late now and the queue doesn't seem to end. I'm not very hopeful that we may reach before time.'

'Don't worry, Didi. We'll take the shortest possible route. We'll reach in, say about, twenty-five minutes,' he suggested.

Sharmila leaned back as she tried to relax. She flipped the book open and muttered the chords in her mind. *C Am Em Am.*

The golden rays of the sun were beginning to fade away. The driver stopped the engine and this made her heart beat faster. He gave a muted sigh of exasperation. She thought about informing the show organizers. It was already five minutes that the taxi was stuck in that terrible traffic.

'One for five rupees and fifty paise. Didi, take one please,' a little girl appeared near the window. Her cracked voice made her sound bigger than she looked. She was in a long, loose frock that was torn in various places. Her dirty hair was falling on her face. Her tired eyes, bad skin and pale face showed her poverty. She was selling masks of animals, clowns and ghosts. She was carrying them in a small bag, with one of the strings snapped, that was hanging down her shoulder. She had three different kinds of mask in her hand for display. The masks, made out of plastic, were artistic combinations of blue, green, red, orange and yellow with black outlines.

'Hey girl!' the taxi driver rudely interrupted her, 'Leave from here! Go!'

'No wait,' Sharmila said.

She had no intention of buying those masks, but there was something in that little girl which made her stop the child before she moved on to the next car. She looked at her, a strange kind of endurance radiated out of her eyes. The girl smiled and her eyes were hopeful.

'What's your name, little girl?' Sharmila asked casually. She had to raise her voice so she could be heard through the noise on the road.

'Titli...'

'Titli! What a beautiful name! Who's kept it for you? Your mother, I suppose.'

'It is my mother's name,' she softened her voice, closing her eyes briefly, and opening again.

'That's strange! So how would you understand if I called your mother by this name that I'm not actually calling you?'

'I don't have a mother. People say that she'd left me when I was very small and went to live with another man. Since then this has become my name,' she said and smiled at me, 'Please Didi take this one,' she said impatiently.

'I will. Where do you stay?'

'There Didi, behind the lamp post,' she said pointing to the next lane, 'on that footpath.'

Sharmila looked at her and wondered if she was living her life bearing her mother's name to remind her, every moment, of the injustice her mother had showed towards her or some kind of revenge, anger or just to give her the feeling of the pure form of a mother's love. Maybe, it gives her a virtual realization that her mother is always with her like her name.

'You live with your father then! You've got siblings?'

'I don't know about my father. People say that he lives in Phoolbangan with his new wife and children. I have no siblings, no one has ever told me about my siblings.'

'So you haven't seen any of them?'

'My mother left me after I was born. I had lived with my

father for few years till he started living with his new family. I was brought back to that old lane where I was born.'

'So who takes care of you?'

'No one cares. I live with my friends. Some of them are like me, without parents, some have parents, and we all live together there,' she pointed to the lane again. Sharmila rolled her eyes across her face. She thought of her own childhood and how much it was different from Titli's. Sharmila realised that she grew up without knowing that such a harsh world as Titli's exists.

'How old are you, Titli?'

'How much will that be? Eight or ten...'

'Do you know the difference between eight and ten?' Sharmila asked, waggling her eyebrows at her.

'How would I, Didi,' Titli said, covering her mouth to giggle slightly, 'you must be kidding. Have I ever been to school?'

'But when you see small children walking to school every morning don't you feel like joining them? Don't you wish to make more friends and learn things with them?'

'No Didi, I don't,' she looked away to see the traffic light. It was still red. The protesting bunch of people had almost cleared the road and gradually the noise disappeared in the air.

'But why? Don't be shy. I know someone who runs an NGO where you could get free education, Titli. Think about it, you wouldn't have to do all this for money.'

'No Didi. I don't wish for so much. I don't want to go to school and learn new things like other children. I only want to hold my mother's hand like they do when they go to school. I dream of it every day. I imagine clutching my mother's hand with my fingers between hers.' Sharmila fixed her eyes on hers as she felt her blood running cold.

The cars from behind started blowing the horns. The traffic light was green. People on the road were getting impatient.

'Didi! The signal is green!'

'Here,' Sharmila said taking the coins out of her purse, 'take your money and keep any three masks you wish to play with.'

Titli kept staring at Sharmila. 'You mean to say they're all mine?' her eyes twinkled.

'Yes they are, Titli.'

The taxi began to move. Titli's little fingers touched Sharmila's. The tiny tips were hard...hardened from the tough reality of her life and its harshness maybe, she thought. For a moment, Sharmila wondered again if Titli was using her name to feel the presence of her mother all the time or was it reminding her of her mother's infidelity every moment so that she could live in her anger for her. May be, she thought, it was a child's empty dream to hold her mother's name, at least, if not her hands...like her empty title. Sharmila looked back, outside the window. Titli was waiting by the road for the signal to turn red. She gradually lost sight of her as the taxi regained its speed.

7

The Old Giant

Khokon managed to come out of the crowded local train.

'Bhai! *Ei je ami ekhane.* I'm here!' He looked around expectantly, only to bring himself back to reality, like a slap on his face that Bindoni was dead. Two quick teardrops ran down his sunburnt cheek as he remembered his elder sister. The Thakurnagar platform was filled with passengers, vendors and fruit sellers. '*Chollish taka kilo...*Mangoes! Rs 40 per kg!'

Khokon tried to make his way out of the stubborn crowd of sweaty people, drenched in salty fragrance. The vans waited outside the platform in a straight queue.

'I'll go to Babupara. Babupara *jabo,*' Khokon raised his voice and booked a van. The van was a set of long and narrow wooden planks that were nailed together behind the driver's seat. There was no handle or anything to which the passengers could seek support from for balance. The passengers and their luggage were stuffed on the wooden planks like a huge single bale of cotton tied together. The ones sitting on the edges had their legs hanging down freely.

Morning had just set in. The tall trees on either side of the narrow road stooped down like a sign of mourning. Shops were beginning to open for the day.

'*Ei Binu Didi! Ekta mishti kine de na re!* Please buy me a sweet,' Khokon once said on a similar morning when his mother, Sarala, had asked both of them to get some rice from a nearby grocery shop. Binodini was ten years old and Khokon was six.

'But Ma has given us money to buy rice, Bhai.'

'I'm sure there will be money left for a sweet.'

'Okay Bhai. Come, I'll buy you one.'

Babu Da's *Mishtanno Bhander* was the best sweet shop in Thakurnagar. Khokon and Binodini walked to the shop. The air was filled with the sizzling noise from the frying *kochuris* in the huge, thick, circular, deep, black cooking pots. Babu Da fried kochuris but sweets were what made him famous. As they stepped inside the shop, the big and juicy *roshogollas* and *jilepis* stored inside glass cabinets filled their mouths with water.

'*Aree* Khokon! At this hour in the morning!' Babu Da said.

'Yes. Ma wants some rice.'

'And Binu? How are your music lessons coming up?'

'Oh they're going good. However, lately I've stopped taking them. Ma says that I will never go to music classes again,' Binodini sighed.

'Why is it?'

'It's because she wants me to look after Bhai and help her in her work after my classes in school.'

'*Bah!* No work is small. It's good to help your mother but you have such a melodious voice, Binu.'

'Don't worry Babu Da. I'll learn all I can by listening to the radio. I love to listen to the radio and Ma doesn't stop me.' Their mother had realised that Binodini knew enough music to bring her well-to-do relations for marriage. She was happy. Binodini knew there was no end to learning. She was determined.

'And which sweet do you want now?' she asked.

'Didi,' Khokon said, 'the *ledikeni*.'

The ledikeni looks partly like a *pantua* and partly like a *langcha*, both famous Bengali sweets. Yet, it tastes quite different from both. Binodini kept staring at Khokon as the soft pieces of ledikeni from the *shaalpata* plate melted in his mouth. The delight in her brother's eyes delighted her and she too desired to taste it.

'*Ei ja!*' Khokon said, 'There is nothing left for you, Didi. I'm so sorry.'

Binodini kissed her brother on his forehead and said, 'Did you enjoy it?'

'Yes Didi! It was so good! Thank you!'

'But don't tell Ma about it.'

'Of course I won't. You're my best sister.' Binodini smiled at Khokon.

Khokon smiled, staring at the bright blue sky as the van now moved past Babu Da's sweet shop.

'*Aree* Khokon *na*? You're Khokon right?' Khokon turned to see Mithu, his childhood friend, sitting behind him on the same van.

'Mithu!'

'I've heard the news of Binodini. It's sad.'

Khokon looked down at the wheels of the van.

'Hey I'm seeing you after almost a decade. *Boudi kemon ache?* Where is your wife and children?'

'They'll come in the afternoon.'

'So you've become an affluent doctor in Kolkata now! Why don't you think of improving the Thakurnagar Hospital? It was built by your father after all.'

'*Dekhi.* Let's see.'

'But Khokon. Though I mustn't say this, but I can't stop myself. You've become successful in your field. Couldn't you take care of your sister? I mean, in the last few days she had become completely schizophrenic. She was even called mad...in public. It obviously hurts to see her in such a state who otherwise could have a promising career in music, had she not met that bastard. Dhiman spoilt her life.'

'Mithu please. I already feel terrible about it. It's not that I haven't tried, you see. Binu Didi was so stubborn always. With great difficulty I had managed to convince her to accept the monthly money that I used to send her. She is...was always very determined that she shouldn't be in debt from anyone...even if it was her younger brother.'

The van stopped at the huge iron gate of the Shuprotik Villa. The gate was open. The red grills on it were now rusted. Cobwebs had gathered around the iron railings. The huge dilapidated house stood before his eyes like a huge giant burdened with the load of age. The giant had gulped his mother, father and now his sister inside its walls where they all breathed their last. The yellow paint on the walls that he had seen ten years back had faded away leaving only dark patches everywhere. The courtyard was filled with people...neighbors, distant friends and relatives, surrounding Binodini's lifeless body. Her long and curvy eye lashes were still. Her beautiful locks of hair were moving slightly with the air, sometimes touching her red lips. She looked beautiful in her death.

She seemed lively in her lifeless being. Khokon could almost see her waking up from sleep and going to college. He could visualize his Binu Didi from twenty years back. Binodini never had a formal education in music before college. She learnt music by listening to the radio and bit by bit polished her skills.

'But you've got no training in music,' Mrs. Mitra, the principal of the Music College said as she looked at her profile.

'But I can sing, Ma'am. I will not disappoint you. I promise,' Binodini put her hands together on the huge wooden table and pleaded. Mrs. Mitra, looked through her thick rimmed glasses and said in a stern voice, 'Go ahead.'

Binodini was tensed. Just before she began, she remembered the words of her mother, 'it's always good to be tensed. It means you feel things. Feelings are important for making good music.' The shabby old curtains let inside a faint light from the sun that shone the wrinkles on the face of Mrs. Mitra prominently.

She began...'*Amar praner pore chole gelo ke...*'

The favourite of all teachers, Binodini was very popular in her college. Everyone loved her.

'Many Congratulations, Binodini. Glad to know!' Everyone Binodini knew had congratulated her on the day she got selected by Akashvani Kolkata for her debut radio show and so had Dhiman when he spoke to her for the first time.

'You seem to be very popular...Binodini, that's your name, right?'

'Yes, I'm Binodini Mullik.'

'I'm honoured to talk to you.'

'Okay speak later. Nice to meet you...you are?'

'Dhiman. Dhiman Mandal from first year, Bengali Honours.'

One year passed in fame and celebrations. Binodini was on her way for a nice and refreshing morning walk on a day which looked so promising. Her navy blue sari veiled her slender form beautifully, the end moved with the wind and she tried her best to keep it in position. Suddenly, thick, dark clouds covered the sky and soon heavy rain began to pour down. She quickly ran and took shelter under a roadside empty hut. Pitter-patter...pitter-patter...

Binodini's heart was humming – *Ai brishti jhepe...dhaan debo mepe...*

Pitter-Patter Pitter-Patter and *ai brishti jhepe...dhaan debo mepe* had blended into each other so smoothly that everything, even the dark sky and the wet sari seemed so perfect. Binodini's heart began to dance with the unbelievably great combination of the two.

'Hello Madam,' a voice interrupted the moment. It was Dhiman at the door. Binodini's smooth black eyebrows were raised and her deep brown eyes glittered in joy and ecstasy. It had been almost a year that they were in love with each other.

Khokon was standing, dumbstruck. The sun shone brightly on both the wrinkles near Binodini's lips. He stood still, perhaps, overpowered by the shadow of the huge giant he was standing before. The Shuprotik Villa kept staring at Khokon in pain, in objection, in search of love and in pangs of death. The smooth black eye brows that were raised and the deep brown eyes which glittered with joy and ecstasy were now still. Her lips were dry and her face was pale. A fly sat on her forehead. Tears ran down his eyes as he kept staring at the place where Binodini grew up reciting:

Kumor parar gorur hari
Bojhai kora kolshi gari

and Sarala, their mother, would correct her:

Kumor parar gorur gari
Bojhai kora kolshi hari

It was raining hard. Binodini was completely drenched. She rubbed her hair while she noticed Dhiman's eyes watching her...the drops of rain that ran down the smooth white skin of her hands...down her red lips...down her neck...down the cleavage that was slightly visible. He didn't miss a single drop. He watched them all as he slowly walked to her.

'You're beautiful.'

'What a surprise, Dhiman! How did you find me?'

'I've more surprise to give you, dear.' Dhiman was now very close to Binodini. Her hair moved with his warm breath. His hands touched her face and then her hair. 'Oh dear! You're wet!'

Dhiman kissed her neck and slowly sucked the rain water dripping down as he unpinned her sari. Gradually, he undraped her and opened his own shirt. His bare chest was sticking to her blouse-veiled breasts. His eyes met hers. Her lips went on his. She closed her eyes.

Dhiman opened the first hook of her blouse. She raised her hand to interrupt him. 'Shh!' he said placing his finger on her lips.

Her blouse was lying at one corner of the small hut. Water was dropping from the thatched roof that was accumulating beside where they were lying. She gifted herself completely to him as he held her breasts, kissed her throughout. She let him inside her deepest core. She knew that she was in love with him and this was the greatest knowledge for her, above all.

One month later, monsoon was over and the sun was shining brightly in the blue sky. The strong smell of mustard had tied the Shuprotik Villa in its mighty shackles of aroma. Binodini opened her eyes. There was a deep brown *Baluchari* sari on her bed and a box of jewelry. The dark green window grills were shining.

Listen Binodini. Akhilesh and his family have spoken to your father. They're coming to see you. This phase of life comes to everybody. Okay?' she suddenly remembered the stern words of her mother. The day had arrived.

A black crow sat on the window and called out in loud

acclamation of something...may be the bright sunny day...may be its vigour, freshness and enthusiasm...or may be the system that the society has been tied to. It looked around in search of life maybe and then it flew away leaving the responsibility of life and the ill-fated society to Binodini.

'Binodini,' Sarala said as she entered Binodini's room, 'you haven't left your bed yet? Look at you. They have come. Get ready! Fast!'

Binodini could hear her father, Surendra and Khokon and few unknown voices. She had nothing in her mind. Her head had stopped working. She did not know what she was doing or about to do. She did as her mother said.

She stood in front of the mirror while Sarala helped her with her jewelry. The black of her eye lashes merged with the kajal. The deep brown eyes did not glitter in joy or ecstasy.

'There you are,' Sarala exclaimed as she adjusted the necklace and looked at Binodini's reflection in the mirror, 'my little princess. You look so beautiful.' Binodini smiled back at her.

In the hall, there were grand arrangements. The sweet, serene smell of the rajnigandha flower had taken the atmosphere in its powerful, intoxicating grasp. The house maids wereserving tea in white cups and trays full of Bhim Chandra Nag's *gurershandesh* and Babu Da's *roshogolla*.

'Arre Akhilesh!' Bipin exclaimed as he took a sip from his cup, 'don't be shy. Take more sweets! Forget about your diabetes today.' Akhilesh was a jolly man and a typical Bengali, food lover. And when it came to sweets...who could stop him! He would forget about all his ailments.

'Don't you dare challenge me in having sweets!' Akhilesh replied, 'challenging Akhilesh Ganguly in terms of gurershandesh and roshogolla is nothing but foolishness. This does look like Bhim Chandra Nag's. Doesn't it?'

'In my twenty-four years of marriage,' exclaimed Nirmala, Akhilesh's wife, 'I could never control his love for sweets.' Nirmala was very much unlike Sarala. She had her origins in Punjab and always carried her Punjabi culture along in her speech, attire and looks. Her thick, long hair was neatly plaited and beautifully decked with golden clips. She was wearing a gorgeous pink and orange salwar kameez. Her green glass bangles were clinking each time she raised her hands to take a sip of the tea.

Nikhil, Nirmala and Akhilesh's son, was sitting quietly with his clean shaven face red in shyness. He wore a white formal shirt and grey pants. He looked up as Binodini took small and tender steps down the stairs. He was blinded by her shimmering beauty. Binodini sat down beside Khokon on the sofa.

Bhenge mor ghorer chabi niye jabi ke amare
O bondhu amar
Na peye tomar dekha eka eka din je amar kaate na re
(Who will break the locks of my house and take me from hence?
In your absence my lonely days do not pass)...Binodini's heart sang.

'Beautiful!' Nirmala said, 'you describe the Bengali beauty...it's almost as if I've begun to envy you already!' Binodini looked at her. She had to smile. She couldn't let her eyes, her face reflect how she felt. She wanted to run away to Dhiman. She felt that she was deceiving everyone in the house. She was helpless.

'But Binodini,' said Akhilesh, 'there was no need for you to be so formal with us. You have taken so much trouble early in the morning. There should be no formalities from now on. Okay! We've come to see the true Binodini.'

Akhilesh's words gave Binodini some kind of encouragement. She wanted to show them her true self, that she was in love with Dhiman, that she was expecting his child and that she couldn't marry anyone else. And when she did speak her mind out silence engulfed the house. Khokon, Sarala, Surendra...they all stared at her in disbelief. After the guests had left in silence Binodini was told to leave the Shuprotik Villa.

'Ma! Binu Didi is lying near Sujoy Babu's pond,' Khokon screamed as he came running home from school, a week later.

'Khokon!' Surendra said, 'did I not say that we won't talk about her inside this house?'

'She's lying unconscious, Baba.'

'So? Where was she for a week?'

'Please!' Sarala said, 'Khokon! Take me to her.'

Sunlight seeped diamond-shaped through the leaves of the trees that lined the Thakurnagar Hospital.

'No...Dhiman...I want to bring up the baby. I can't let our child die!' Binodini couldn't say anything other than these words. Her eyes were wide and frightful. Her hair was unruly and she was restless. It seemed as if she had to tell a lot of things to the world and was trying hard to express herself.

They learnt that Binodini was raped and tortured and the life that was growing up inside her was dead. She was no longer as lively as she used to be. She stopped singing forever. They brought her back to the Shuprotik Villa.

One month passed. Khokon went to Kolkata to pursue higher studies. The Shuprotik Villa, the old giant, where his parents had breathed their last, had taken Binodini away as well.

Khokon gazed at her dead body. He put down his suitcase and walked towards her slowly. Sitting beside her, he could see the tapering design of the embroidery on her sari that peeped out of the white cloth that covered her. The part of the sari was a beautiful maze of golden threads, little glass pieces and sequins. There was a very narrow space between the threads and sequins for the cloth to breathe. It was his mother's, he recalled.

8

The Sky Blue Steps

The long sky blue steps marked the entrance of the house. That's where they used to rest in the evenings, Mili and Tutu. And when the stars gradually appeared in the darkness and Mukul *Dadu's* coconut tree started scaring Mili, Tutu would laugh aloud at her sister's meaningless fear of a *Mecho Bhoot* or a fish – eating ghost sitting on the tree. Then Ma would call, 'Mili, Tutu, come inside and finish your homework.'

After they finished their homework, Tutu would sit to practice her music lessons on the harmonium. Mili would quietly walk up to her sister and sit beside her.

Aloker ei jhornadharay dhuiye dao...
(Pour your cascades of sunshine
Bathing, steeping me in gold
Let layers of dust wash away
Touch awake a slumbering soul...)

Her melodic voice would draw silence everywhere. Neighbours took a pause from everything they would be doing to listen to Tutu. Just then Baba would return from work. The sweetness that Tutu's song brought around would take off the day's exhaustion.

'Tutu, lovely song dear. Why don't you teach your sister too?'

Tutu looked at Mili...Mili's eyes were twinkling and she was very excited.

'Come Mili, let's try this. Sing, Sa...Re...Ga...' And Tutu and Mili would sing along through the evening. They would sway in the mild wind that entered through the south window when Ma and Baba would come and sit beside them.

Often, Ma would tell them to help her offer the morning prayers. After their baths the two of them would pick flowers. Split bamboo canes fenced their yard. Trees, long and short, lined inside the yard along the fence...rose, mango, coconut and many more. Tutu, being elder by four years, was taller and it was she who actually did the flower picking. Mili always tagged along with her elder sister. If Tutu picked the flowers, Mili would carry the flower basket to collect them. And then they would spread a mat under their mango tree and engage in lazy morning conversation, eating berries.

'Do you like Moni Didi? I met her yesterday on my way back from school. She was saying girls get married and go to another house and then the new house becomes their own house. She said she was going to get married and that one day you and I too will.'

'That is so ruthless of her!'

'But then I thought again if it is true. It must be, that's how we've seen our elder cousin sisters get married.' She turned towards Mili and continued, 'One day when I'll get married to someone will this house no longer be mine, will things no more be the same, will we no longer sit like this in the afternoons and chatter away endlessly?'

Mili stared at her sister. Her eyes widened as Tutu spoke. She hugged her sister and said, 'Never, I'll save you from getting married. I'll hide you somewhere.'

'Mili! You're so silly! We all must get married but I feel things shouldn't change after that.'

'But I'll miss you when you're gone. What will I do in the afternoons? Who will help me pick the flowers?'

Ma was standing behind them all the while Tutu and Mili discussed about marriage and the life after. Ma looked at both of them but said nothing. She moved her hand over Mili's and Tutu's heads and walked inside.

In the evening, the air would be heavy with the fragrance of the *shiuli* flowers. Ma always made hot tea and snacks in the evening. Light conversation would toss all around...bring a little honey tomorrow, Tutu is getting taller, we are short of candles, next month is Khuku's marriage, need to buy something for her, etc. Occasionally, heavy discussions came up like politics in Baba's office, that onion price has gone up and there is too much crime these days, where are all the values and morals? Ma would then lose herself in her favorite novel by Sarat Chandra Chatterjee or Tagore.

Ma was strict about a few things. Though she never stopped Mili and Tutu from having fun, she wanted the girls to have some discipline and not roam around like grazing cows in the fields of Shankar Dadu. She showed them the pleasure of having tamarind in the lazy summer afternoons, read out stories and opened the huge world of classics and songs and dramas by Tagore. But at the same time, she was very particular about the girls returning home by seven in the evening.

It was a wintry Wednesday and it was raining hard. Winters are generally dry and dull and very cold. That day, the clouds thundered and poured at will. It was wet and raining and much colder. It rained and rained. Tutu and Mili were stuck in the rain on their way back from tuition classes and the seven in the evening rule was broken. They increased their speed past the shops big and small that were beginning to shut down, struggling to keep the maroon umbrella in position against the wind. The big drops of water were striking with force, almost hurting them. Blinded by the rain, they could faintly see Ma and Baba, standing on the long sky blue steps. The water had drowned the first two steps and was almost touching the third. They quickly walked up the steps with hearts beating fast, knowing that Ma was angry. They returned home but only after half-past-eight at night.

'Come, come, come,' Ma said, 'Give me the umbrella and take this towel. It's raining like cats and dogs today.'

'Yes Ma,' said Mili, 'it started just before classes got over and the roads have become water logged.'

'We were so worried!'

That day Tutu and Mili realised that in worry and relief, Ma and Baba had always nurtured love and trust for them.

And thus, the years passed. Moni Didi, from the next lane, brought news of a suitable groom for Tutu. Soon, things were finalized and a date was fixed for her marriage. Tutu was happy because she now understood that she was supposed to be happy. The idea of having a new home pleased her. The old conversation under the mango tree with Mili was faded from her memory. But Mili was sad that she was going away.

The wedding went off smoothly. Tutu was now married and was not staying in the same house with Mili. She was settled in Mumbai. Tutu looked enthused in her new life. Ma would tearfully remember her in the evenings when it would be time for her to sing. The silence in the house seemed disturbing, but it was Mili who was affected the most. The celebrations of the wedding brought Mili momentary excitement, but shortly after, she yearned to be with her sister again. She remembered the endless chats when they were very small. The good times, those which were filled with fun and laughter and joy and happiness... she started missing them.

It was April and Tutu was visiting them for the first time after she settled down in Mumbai. Mili had her final tests in college and did not get to speak to her properly. She glanced at Tutu from time to time. She looked so different! The vermilion, the conch shell bangles, wearing a sari like mothers did all day...everything had changed about her, she thought. She was hurt, there was emptiness surrounding her. There was a huge round dot on her forehead...just like a moon. Tutu was somewhat pensive and silent for a while.

'You look so beautiful!' Mili said to start a conversation.

'Mili! You've grown taller! Taller than me.'

Mili could barely suppress her tears from rolling down. Tutu was being so upsettingly formal with her. Where is the sweet and loud and enthused sister she grew up with, she wondered. 'How's Mumbai?'

'Mumbai is different! It's busy, it's dusty, it's posh, it's different from everything I've ever known. You can barely see the sky, hidden behind the tall buildings, the moon seems so detached, the trees look indifferent and distant.'

'You've liked the new city so far?'

'I'm not sure, you know. I used to be so scared sometimes. What if the city wouldn't be good to me? I think now I might have begun to like the place.'

Mili expected Tutu to say otherwise. She was happy and sad, a strange combination of contrasting feelings. She knew once Tutu started loving Mumbai the faint hope of coming back home would be gone forever. She couldn't imagine a land with hidden sky, detached moon and aloof trees. The place where they grew up singing songs, picking flowers and having tamarind was so close to nature, to the two of them, for all these years. 'Do you sing?' she asked.

'I do. But no one asks me to sing, no one really has that time, I said, it's a busy place. So I sing for my own pleasure. I hum while I do the household work.'

For a while they were silent. Mili tried to lighten her mind and said, 'So that means you never know, the moment you start singing aloud you might sound like Shankar Dadu's cows!'

The two sisters couldn't stop giggling. They discussed *vada pav*, traffic, slums, buildings, and other things in Mumbai.

A year passed. Mili was almost seventeen now and started going to college. She was growing up into a beautiful, elegant lady. Everyone loved her for her sweet and sober nature. One could sit before her for hours, listening to her innocent yet graceful words. She would sit with the harmonium to sing but that would only bring back Tutu's memories and her voice would tremble.

Mili had friends in college but her best friend was Ma. She felt that only Ma understood what she felt when Tutu was married to another man. She found solace around Ma. Ma was also very fond of her. Ma would accompany her now for having tamarind and berries under their mango tree. Mili was now taller and picked flowers herself, missing Tutu all the while.

Mili often thought about the immaterialities of nature. The lovely abstract spring flowers and their soft pink colour would make her view life in a much simpler form. She viewed nature as a beholder of an immense treasure of wealth and pleasure.

Thus two winters passed, another arrived. Moni Didi, from the next lane, was bringing in suitable grooms for Mili. At first she had not taken any notice, but as discussions about her marriage became regular she felt like she was on an extended probation. She was very disturbed with all these developments. She would think a lot and try to understand but everything failed her attempt to find out why things had to happen so fast...she was already staying away from Tutu and now she would have to leave her parent's home. She didn't like the idea. It was as if everything around her was running, leaving her way behind and she simply couldn't cope up. She felt like being at the crossroads. She sensed the world around her preparing for a new lane...her new life. Inevitable though this was, she hoped that this stretched parole would keep getting extended.

Mili did not think about nature anymore. The immaterialities of nature did not amuse her. She didn't even notice the spring flowers and their soft pink colour.

On a winter afternoon, she reclined on the sky blue steps. She folded her legs and rested her arms on her knees. She looked at Mukul Dadu's coconut tree. It had been years since that the tree had stopped frightening her. She slowly put her head down on her hands and closed her eyes. Gradually, thick clouds covered the sky. Mili felt few drops of water on her feet. 'Ah Tutu! Stop throwing water on me!' She opened her eyes and realised that it was only rain that was spattering the sky blue steps.

9

When the Trunk Creaks

That Sunday afternoon the weather was surprisingly pleasant. It had been a particularly bad winter with a mild sun and uncomfortably cold winds. It seemed like the sun was back in its agitation and it was charming. It's always delightful to sleep in the backyard of the house on such winter afternoons.

✦

A year was gone since our marriage and Jhimli had, weakly, begun regarding me as her husband. Marriages in our village took place without the consent of the bride, regardless of her priorities. Before marriage, Jhimli and I lived in the same village and she stayed close to our house. I enjoyed watching her from a comfortable distance as she would be drying her long wavy hair in the sun, sitting in the lawn with her sisters when I returned from college. Her dupatta lying on the grass, would show her cleavage slightly from the neck of her *kurti*. She was still in school then.

'But I don't want to marry!' she had said stubbornly. I wanted to. I had secretly loved her golden skin, dark eyes and curly hair for years. I heard her conversing with her mother inside their small bedroom while I waited outside. Her father left me alone and rushed inside.

'He's a kind hearted man. He'd not be cruel to you. He's the best you can get.'

'But...but I can't marry anyone!' she burst out.

'Why not, girl? Do you have a lover?' I listened carefully.

'I want to study. I want to go to college, become a doctor. These are my dreams!' I laughed silently in my mind at her silly audacity. I knew that she was going to be mine.

'No!' her father declared, 'It's just...it's ridiculous! Such things don't happen in our village. We cannot get a better man for you. He is coming to us for free and you're eighteen already. Don't forget you've got sisters to be married. We've got things to arrange. Get ready and come outside. He's waiting for you.' I settled down. Soon, Jhimli appeared in a blue sari. She glared at me, breathing heavily. We didn't speak to each other. Two weeks later we got married.

We spent our first night in her house. The room was decorated with flowers and candles. She was sitting, bundled up in her red sari and decked with jewellery. I proceeded towards her, already excited about the idea of finally getting her close to me.

'You're here?' she looked at me and said. The candle light looked faint before her austerity. 'I feel that you married me for your own motives and those motives are your own business,' she added hastily, 'and that I have no claim on you and you on me. You're at perfect liberty to behave as you wish and let me do so too. If you find someone else, I won't stand in your way. But I cannot be a good wife, all I wanted is to see my parents happy and my sisters married. I want to work, earn money and study medicine,' she finished lamely. The blood was visibly hot in her cheeks and I could almost see her ears burning.

I felt my ears burning as well, and so was the rest of me from the neck up. I felt my eyes flaming slightly. Women in our village did as we men told them. That's how I've grown up seeing my mother and then my brother's wife.

'At liberty to behave as I wish?' I said, 'And you'll not stand in my way. Have you become insane?' I bent to pull off my shoes and then picked them up and threw them, one after another, as hard as I could, at the wall. I had dreamt of this night with her for years and now she just couldn't spoil everything.

I glared at her. She was staring at my shoes expressionlessly. 'So you've no claim on me, Jhimli? You'll free me to take my pleasure where I like, is that it? Well, is it?' I demanded.

'Well, yes,' she said, moving slightly backward, 'That's what I meant.' I sat on the bed in front of her and grabbed her arms. She jerked.

'Well, if you've no claim on me, Jhimli,' I said, 'I have on you! Come here.' I took her candle lit face in my hands and set my mouth on hers. I put my weight hard against hers, my hands pinned her shoulders to the bed.

'What do you...' she began, but I ducked my head and kissed her, cutting her short as she fought against it, trying to pull back from me. I thrust my tongue inside her mouth, revolving and plunging, retreating and plunging again. I bent and scooped her up with an arm under her knees, ignoring her attempts to get down.

'Let go of me!' she said. 'What do you think you're doing?'

'Well, I thought that that was reasonably clear, Jhimli.' I lowered my head. The clear gaze from her wide eyes pierced me. 'Though, if you want me to describe it fully to you, I want to make love with you now, and keep doing that till you've learnt just what claim I have on you.' And I kissed her again, deliberately hard, cutting off her protests.

'I don't want to sleep with you!' she said, when at last I freed her mouth.

'I didn't intend to sleep with you either, Jhimli. Not just yet. Perhaps tomorrow, when I'm not tired and ready to pay thorough attention to you.'

'You know very well what I mean!' her eyeballs rolled at my face, 'I don't want to make love with you ever!' she said, lying down with her fists balled at her sides.

'I didn't ask your preference for that matter, Jhimli,' I lowered my voice with my face sufficiently close to hers that I could smell her sweet breath, 'You're my wife, and if I want you, Jhimli, then I'll have you.'

A year passed. Gradually, she surrendered and I made love to her at my own free will, beginning by moving my fingers round and round on her thighs or her neck or sometimes below her ears and then our eyes met and my lips touched hers. I was a proud father, proud that I had a son. My neighbours called me fortunate for this. They always said that boys are here to stay, girls are always to go away.

It wasn't easy, though. Jhimli and I prayed for a son in temples around the village for about a year. I can recall the night before our son was born. I had told Jhimli that it had to be a son or we wouldn't have it. Jhimli slowly caressed her stomach and said that she had feelings that she had a boy inside her.

The sun felt enchanting and I fell asleep in the comfortable weather. Jhimli had been busy all day. She was worked up always after our son was born, a month back...she would stay up all night feeding the baby every two hours, changing the wet clothes, washing this and scrubbing that. No one in the village had known of someone called a governess or a nanny then, though it is not that many know now, but some families have begun liking the idea of a baby sitter.

Months back, on a similar delightful afternoon I was in the backyard. I wasn't taking a nap. I was simply lying with my eyes closed and thinking about my still unborn son. Jhimli's stomach was really big and the baby inside had begun responding to tickling. Jhimli and I would laugh every time he did that and each time he did, I revelled in the strength of my masculinity. A sudden gush of hot wind ran across me that had made me a little uncomfortable. I could hear the creaking noise of the door that opened to the backyard. The leaves made a vigorous rustling noise as the wind moved against the large standing mango tree. The trunks made a discrete chirr for longer than I had imagined it would. Another quick and short wind passed by, throwing down something soft and puffy on my face. I fell disgusted with the continuous interruption of my leisure moment. I picked it up from my face and threw it on the other side of the yard. It was an ugly little bird. A grey and white large cat seemed to be waiting for it. Its eyes sparkled like a couple of green gems and with a faintly audible howl it promptly picked up the bird in its mouth and ran towards a corner. A large murder of crows started calling out like they do about dusk every night. It was loud and crazy. I opened my eyes. The crows made an M-shape among them. Perhaps this makes them a murder of crows, the first letter of murder and not a group or a herd, I thought. I turned towards my right side and slept and dreamt about my son.

✦

I woke up suddenly with a quick puff of wind that went past me. I heard my wife. She was screaming. I sensed fear in her trembling voice. I ran inside to see her. She was sitting on the floor and crying. The neighbours had gathered in front of our little hut. Our son's cradle was empty.

'What is it? What's the matter?'

'Our son, our son. A fox carried him away inside its mouth, such a cruel, wicked fox,' Jhimli looked at me and cried.

'I saw the fox running towards the bushes in the east,' one of the neighbours said.

My ears were burning. I could feel a thrust of hot blood rushing on my face. I caught Jhimli's hair which she left open and pulled it hard making her head hang sideways and said, 'You whore! Where were you when this happened?'

Just then I heard the creaking noise. The trunk of the mango tree moved in the wind. The crows were calm. A shiver ran down my spine. I left Jhimli's hair and clutched my own.

10

Rainbows in the Grass

I swung down the road this evening towards 17, Russel Street, to meet Sandy at his house. His housekeeper answered the door, a tall stringy woman with strands of neatly combed grey hair running down from her head and tied into a round bun. She welcomed me in and towed me down a long, narrow and dark hallway to his room, which, by contrast, was blinding with light from the huge windows that ran almost from the ceiling to the floor in one wall. The bright blue curtains were left half open to show the beautiful evening sky.

I looked around the room. It had been thoroughly trashed. A piercing screech from behind made me jump. There was a parrot clock above the curtain rail.

'Good evening!' Sandy said from behind.

'You should keep this devil of a clock somewhere else. My heart almost skipped a beat.'

Sandipan Roy has been my best friend since I was very little. We grew up in the same lane. I looked around the place. It was a scene of wreckage. The Saturday breakfast news was on the TV but he didn't seem to be listening to it and I could make that out because his face looked restless. I sat down on the sofa in front of his bed and started fidgeting with an empty water bottle that I found lying beside me.

'My room doesn't look very good, I know. Mom and Dad aren't

home, so I guess it's got to be this way today.'

'So what have you been doing since morning rather than trashing your room in such perfect manner? Why are you so tense?'

He turned off the news and said, 'I met her today.'

I lifted my face up from the bottle and looked at him inquisitively. 'The girl I met at the food court the other day,' he continued, 'Shruti...she was there at the grocery store this morning. We both were standing next to each other at the payment counter. I was waiting for my turn when I heard her sweet voice.' Sandy walked down the wooden floor and sat down beside me.

'So did you spend some time talking and finding more about each other in a coffee shop or someplace like that?'

'We went for a walk. She didn't like coffee shops it seemed. Her sweet fruity fragrance, I'll never forget!'

He smiled and looked very happy.

'Did you ask her where she stays?'

'I offered to walk her to her home. She lives in the next street.'

'Maybe then we both must've crossed her before, on our way to work or the grocery store.'

'Possible! She's the cutest girl you'll ever come across in his place. In the whole city. I wish she wears a cute baby pink top someday. She would've looked like a doll, with her beautiful brown hair, which she might've chosen to leave open. And boy, it would be just amazing to see her hair fall perfectly across the forehead without even her trying.'

I'd never seen my best friend speak about a girl in such vivid detail. In fact, we barely discussed girls. We both felt uneasy around such topics. I listened to Sandy as he went on to describe her. Clearly, he was serious about this girl and I was very happy for him.

'I want to take her out this weekend,' he continued, pressing my hands heartily.

'Did you ask her out?'

'No I didn't. I'll ask her out tomorrow. She said she comes to the store every morning at 10 a.m. just before it opens. It's just that I'm nervous.' I patted his shoulders as he continued, 'Are you getting bored? Because even if you're, I'm not done yet.'

'What makes you say that, Sandy? I was just thinking that it's really very odd that we're discussing a girl...that too I somehow feel, you're in love with her. We've never had such discussions before. But I'm delighted.'

'I was just dying to talk to someone about her. My stomach was churning like a giant cement mixer since this morning and I too think I'm in love.'

'I'm very happy, Sandy, congratulations...I'm so glad! Please tell me more. Where did you go walking?'

'Well. We didn't spend much time together. It was just from the store to her house. You know, I want to tell her every day that she's so beautiful. Did I mention she's an artist? She's invited me to her exhibition that's next week.'

'Wow! Haven't been to an exhibition for quite some time. I'll come too.'

'Yes, we can always go together. She said she's made a poster where she's used iron-on paints and painted with it on the canvas. It's called encaustic painting she says. She was very excited about the entire thing. When she was talking to me about her passion for artwork I could see her eyes light up. She spoke with so much of vigour and passion.'

'That's something amazing. And did she tell you where she

learnt painting with an iron?'

'She did. She went to an art school where they paint with all kinds of crazy stuff. She said that she knows how to paint with vegetables.'

'That's just beyond me, Sandy!'

'It's beyond my understanding too. I cannot wait to see this girl again.'

'Who all are there in her family? Does she have a little sister so you can talk to her about me?' I winked and smiled at him, 'Well, I was just kidding!'

'She never mentioned about a brother or sister. Her mother, she said, started working in a bank after her father passed away last year. She said that she wants to earn money through her artwork since her mother works overtime often to earn a little extra. She seemed to miss her father a lot, she keeps talking about him.'

'How did he die? Did she tell you?

'He had cancer she said, in the lungs. Tears welled up at the corners of her eyes when she mentioned that. She recalled and said she kissed him on his forehead just before he passed away. And that how minutes after he passed she said she realised that she had not kissed her father since she was a little girl. The way she spoke about her father, it was sad. And then I could feel a small tear drop running quickly down my cheeks.'

'She's a very sweet woman. She deserves all the happiness in the world.'

'She's a very caring girl, she worries a lot about her mother's health. This weekend I want to tell her my feelings. I know it's going to be tough for me since she might feel that I barely know her. I'm confident though. She won't let me down, will she?'

'Relax, Sandy. You're getting tensed up again. You want some water?'

There was a jug on the small table near the wall, at a corner. I stood up. He clutched my hand and said, 'Sit down, I don't need water...thanks though. I need you by my side. I've never proposed a girl.'

'Neither have I, but you know what, I feel everything is going to be just fine, Sandy. You want me to help you fix the room? It is in a total mess.'

We adjusted the bed sheet and the pillows and neatly placed the books inside the shelf. Sandy sat down on the bed. I opened the curtain completely. It was a beautiful summer evening. I sat down beside him. This girl has changed him over a conversation, I thought, maybe that's how love happens.

'I've brought you a little bit of refreshment,' the housekeeper announced, setting the tea tray firmly in the center of the table. She looked me over with a curious eye, assessing with a faint glaze over the eyeballs. The grooves on the right side of her mouth had deepened and her brows pressed together in what looked like a trance. She quietly walked out of the room.

'There was,' Sandy said, 'a strong gust of wind for a little while as we walked. Her hair got a little messy and when the flurry was gone she asked me if she was looking okay. I mean that's such a meaningless question. I want to tell her every day that she's so beautiful. There's not a single thing that I'd like to alter in her face, it is perfect the way it is. I told her not to bother even asking that. She gave me a smile and it seemed as if the whole world stopped and stared for that little moment.' The tenderness in his voice was overwhelming.

I watched his smile run away from his face suddenly. He looked onto the floor and continued, 'But there's a slight confusion. I don't know if she likes how I look. And I've got no idea how to figure that out.'

'Why? It should be simple. Ask her, silly.'

'That's not really a very good idea. She can't see. She lost her sight, she said, when she was in the eighth grade. And that's what makes me worried. How would I ever know if she likes the way I look? She didn't mind being legally blind, with only twelve percent of her vision, she said. She said something very beautiful today. She said that after it rains there's usually a dew left on the grass, and because of the way her eyes refract the light, she can see rainbows in the grass. She said she just loves it that way. Now is that not just amazing?'

There was a short pause. Sandy smiled at me and said, 'Look at me...I forgot to share the muffins I got this morning from the grocery store. They're so soft. Shruti says they're amazing, just melt in your mouth, so I got them. Just a second. I kept the box inside the fridge.'

He stretched out his hands. I took the stick, his white cane from near the bed and gave it to him. I watched him as he used the stick for obstacles on his way towards the refrigerator.

In the years we grew up together many times I had seen friends and other kids making fun of Sandy. I always felt sorry for him since I knew that his life would never be the same again after he lost both his eyes in that disastrous road accident when he was eleven. Often I had shown him pity in my mind. On his twelfth birthday, I stood beside him like always when he was about to cut the cake. The house was overflowing with guests and gifts and common friends from the same street. Sandy blew out the candles and closed his eyes to make his wish. When he opened his eyes he was attacked by a roar of laughter.

'Did you wish for another cane, Sandy?' the kids in the party shouted, 'Why do you need to close your eyes? It means the same thing to you.' They made fun of him.

'Friends can be mean sometimes, Sandy,' I whispered in his ears as I noticed his eyes become watery and helped him cut the cake.

I walked to him after the guests were gone. He was sitting alone staring outside his window. 'What did you wish for this year, Sandy?' I asked. We have always shared what we wished for on our birthdays through the years we have known each other.

'When I see people mocking me, I feel very angry and very sad, both at the same time. This year, I wished I could meet someone who could see the world through my eyes.'

Since then he wished the same thing each year. I was happy that his wish, after so many years, had come true.

As he struggled, I heard him say, 'I somehow feel her cane is better than mine. I should ask where I could get one like hers.'

11

Stubborn

I walked down the stairs into the underground hall. Light was shimmering throughout the place and I could see her from a distance. I was seeing her after two, long years. It was a long, narrow room outfitted with tables down the length of each wall. There was a constant stream of waiters and waitresses, dressed in serviceable shades of grey and white for men and only white for women, issuing from archways at either ends of the hall, laden with jugs, trenchers and trays. The rays of early summer's late sunlight came through the narrow windows. Most of the diners kept their eyes on their plates. People ate as they pleased. They were helping themselves from the serving platters. The air was loud with conversation.

The radiant woman was sitting in a wide, open, fresh scented, artificial garden just outside the hall surrounded by vast and spacious, healing light. Was she always so beautiful or was the blue sari making her glamorous? I wondered. It was as if light was radiating out of her. Her proliferating presence was brighter than all the light around us. She was smiling reassuringly as I walked towards her past the pillars and the statues. Where have you been, I thought...you've certainly taken a long time to come back. My thoughts declined as I reconsidered and realised that I was the one who had always been hard headed, she was a perfect woman, always complacent and exactly the way ladies must be.

She stood up. I could see her slender waist through her silk sari. I felt the unstoppable desire to hold her in my arms and kiss her. I yearned to make up for the times we had lost, hating each other. I didn't quite know how to begin.

'Rajesh! How have you been?' Panchali said.

'Good,' I smiled awkwardly, I felt a trifle uneasy, as I often did when I had to be submissive, and said, 'My business has flourished in these two years! How're you?'

'Two years! Rajesh...I thought I might forget how you look.'

'But you didn't, did you?'

'Why? Certainly I didn't...and yes, I'm doing well. It was just today morning, I was going through the wedding photos.'

I looked into her eyes, I saw towering grace and soothing gentleness. I realised the conversation was getting emotional, something I didn't want...or did I? I was confused.

'So what will you have?' I looked into the menu book to withdraw attention from her perfect eyebrows and the curves of her lips.

'Sweet tea?'

I looked up. I was mildly amused. I ordered two sweet tea for us.

'*Sweet tea!*' I said. 'Couldn't forget those long evenings with just sweet tea. Anyway, how's everybody in the family?'

'Papa had a surgery last month. He is doing fine. Mom is good.'

I had nothing to distract attention from her. It was difficult to talk after two years, tougher than I had imagined. She had grown beautiful over the time since I had last seen her.

It was raining heavily that day. Before I dropped her at her office, she said she had a small office party that day and that suggested that she would be late reaching home. When she returned, it was quite late. She tiredly dropped her bag on the bed and took the dressing table seat to face the mirror.

'I sometimes don't understand why you need to work.'

'Rajesh!' she said as she took off her tiny pearl earrings that were radiating their brilliance. I looked at her in the mirror.

'I meant, don't get me wrong, but you come back from your office, visibly exhausted,' I had been extremely possessive about her. Her exhaustion was an excuse, I'd feel a burning sensation inside my chest and my stomach churned whenever she said she would return home late. 'Consider this as my narrow mentality or anything else, I didn't like that chap outside who dropped you in his car. You could've told me, I could've picked you from your office.'

'In that case,' she said practically, 'I expected you to be tired too and I knew I would be late. There were many new interns and it takes time to introduce them to everyone. Besides, I'd told you that I would be late.'

'Well,' I said seriously, 'someone else could've always done that. How much skill does that take anyway?' I sat down at the edge of the bed.

She stared at me from the mirror. She turned and walked towards me. She grabbed my chin and turned my face towards her. She widened her eyes in simulated surprise.

'Are you implying,' she demanded, 'that the man you saw outside was some sort of, of...' she hesitated, looking for the right word, 'romantic interest of mine?' she finished.

'I don't know Panchali,' I hesitantly began, 'well, you know, it was two years, I was abroad. And we saw each other only three times, and all this time you were doing a commendable job, looking after my parents.' I chose my words carefully, 'Do you have a liaison?'

She interrupted this rambling by jerking free. 'Do you think I've been unfaithful to you?' she demanded. 'Do you? Because, Rajesh, if so, you better tell me and leave this room this minute. Leave the house altogether! How dare you imply such a thing?'

'Why should I leave?' I made my point firmly, 'This is my house. If anyone leaves, it's no one else but you. You can go, stay with that chap who dropped you here tonight.'

We didn't talk to each other and went to sleep. The next morning before I woke up, she was gone. She left a note, folded it neatly, beside me, on the bed. It said that she would only be back when I wanted since the house belonged to me. I didn't miss the emphasis on the last part. I was thoroughly angry at this.

Sometimes I feel I could have made things moderately fine. But I was much weaker than I thought I was.

The waiter brought the sweet tea in beautiful white porcelain cups.

'Are you alright?' She asked. I noticed a swallow of tea run visibly own her neck that bore three strands of pearls and disappeared beneath the gleaming beads.

'Ya, yes, And how about your job?' I said.

'It's good. I'd got a promotion six months back. Now I go to the 11 East Street building.'

'Oh! I've shifted my office to a couple of lanes away from your office. Strange, we never crossed each other!'

'Did you visit the Candies Coffee Shop that came up lately?'

'I did, once,' I was a little amazed by her sudden change of subject, 'I barely get time out of work and at night all I want is a good night's sleep.'

'And before you go to sleep do you still watch the Lu Lu Show? I remember you're just crazy about it...like a little kid!'

'Oh don't you tell me that! You fought with me so many times for that stupid Puff Wonders at 11!'

'C'mon...when did I insist?' There was a small pause and then she continued, 'Have you finally started liking cashew nuts? It's so weird that you didn't like cashews.'

'Those little devils! They bloat you up with calories.'

'And from when did you become a conscious calorie taker, Mr. Honeybun?'

I saw a tiny teardrop form at the corner of her eyes. Our college days flashed before my eyes. Whenever I was sad or felt low, Panchali would hug me and say, 'Mr. Honeybun, I'm here always!' She was silent for a long time, staring at the table, once in a while tilting the cup, or rolling it slowly between her slender palms.

'I know what you're thinking. You too had a nick name. I used to call you...call you...'

'Miss Pumpkin Pie!'

'Yes Pie, Pumpkin Pie. Remember once when I called you that in front of the entire class, you got so angry.'

'Yes and I even cried in the girls' room.'

'Girls' room! What, do all girls go cry there? Besides you never told me about it.'

'That's because I didn't want you to give me another name, a Cry Baby or something like that. Let me see,' Panchali looked down under the table.

'What're you searching for?'

'Not searching, silly. I'm checking if you're wearing socks!'

'What the...that was long back when I skipped wearing socks

since they had to be washed. C'mon, stop laughing. I've grown up now.'

'Have you still got the habit of keeping your drinking glass here and there uncovered?'

'I doubt if I've covered it before leaving home this morning.'

'You're still the same, Rajesh. How's Mom?'

'Mom isn't keeping well lately. She's been having issues with diabetes.'

'Does she say anything about me?'

'Not particularly,' I looked at her expecting eyes, 'she mentioned you yesterday when she couldn't find her pills. We have wasted the years in between misunderstanding each other, Panchali.'

'Not as much as you did, Rajesh. I had waited for you every day. I thought you'd come to take me back on reading my note. I was certainly wrong. What made you so stubborn?' I looked into my cup as she spoke the words huskily.

'Mom says that little things in relationships like small stones fuse into one another, and form something like huge, big boulders that can no longer be removed. I believe it isn't a boulder yet,' I looked at her hopefully.

'I've cried for you so much. It was so hard to imagine that you didn't even give a call to ask about me. And I kept wondering where,' she took a short pause and said, 'where did we go wrong, when did we leave back those good days behind. I'd always known that you're one stubborn man. But...' I pressed a finger on her lips.

I said the words that I must have told long back, 'I'm very lonely, Panchali. I want you back. Please, come back with me.' It felt amazing to express the feelings I had buried in my heart for so long. She had always waited for me, I thought, how I wish I did this before.

✦

I took her hands, tucking it snugly beneath my elbow, and we turned towards the parking area. We strolled, hand in hand. I wrapped my hands around her, she stayed stiff, but I persisted, caressing her hair and rubbing her shoulder in the way I knew she liked. And after a long time, I murmured into her hair, 'I know you'd never been unfaithful, you'd never do such a thing. I love you so. Nothing, through the years had stopped me from loving you. It was just, like you call it, I had been stubborn.'

She laughed and looked up, 'And thus I was compelled to wonder, what made you call this dinner tonight.'

A flash heralded a sudden breaking of the storm. A thunder went off as though in answer to her words and it started drizzling. Her hair was wet and I yearned to touch the rain drops on her forehead. She sat beside me, inside the car. The gentle breeze was moving her erratic, wet strands. She was looking outside the window, at the sky. We didn't speak. I was a happy man that evening. I got back all that I'd lost, just that we wasted a lot of time...I had been too stubborn, had always been this way since childhood.

I stopped the car when we reached in front of her house. I slowly moved my hands over hers and said, 'You look wonderful in the moonlight, in the rain. Your hair smells wonderful, your skin glows like ivory.'

She got off the car, her smile lightened. She walked to stand by my window and pressing a kiss on the top of my head she handed me a large envelope. I opened it as I watched her walk away from me. Inside it there were twenty two love letters she had written for me over the last two years. There was a post-it note on the envelope that said, 'Letters I was too stubborn to send.'

12

By-lane Dreamers

The sun was shining on the by-lanes of Kolkata. The footpath emerged with a fresh glow as the winter morning bathed in the rays of the sun. The freshness had brought around an urge for hot black tea in almost every home, lodge and roadside tea stall. Hot black tea with a couple of biscuits tastes like heaven on earth on any winter morning, and when such a morning is drenched and perfectly blended with the golden sunrays, four rupees and fifty paise is nothing but a satisfactory compensation for immense pleasure.

The strong shackles of cold of the rather long night melted into a bright morning, even for the children belonging to the footpath, who can never think of paying the price for a cup of tea. But the towering sun showered its comforting rays without bias on all who wished to seek pleasure from it. Arun and Dipu broke open the shackles of the winter morning to face a new day with new difficulties, new hardships and new stories of livelihood.

'Dipu,' said Arun, rubbing his eyes, 'what shall we do today? I don't like this street, it has no big buildings that I can see and dream of having my own, and very few cars take this road, and no friends in the lanes nearby.'

Dipu yawned loudly and kept sitting on the torn blanket. He took the paper ball and rolled it repeatedly. The ball was their only mode of entertainment...their toy, their joy, their frustration, their destitution. Arun stared at the ball as it went up and down.

'Let's do something different today,' cried Dipu, 'today we'll work harder and earn double.' The road was slowly getting filled with cars honking and the air was getting heavier. Arun was confused and could make nothing out of Dipu's suggestions. His rough, round face wore a frown. He looked at Dipu, scratching his torn and dirty shirt.

'Have you heard of the new park?' asked Dipu, 'The new one for children near the next crossing? I've heard it has a very funny name. They say it's called the Nicco Park. Let's go there today. I get bored playing with these paper balls. We'll return before Aunt is back.'

'But where will we get money from? They ask money for entering these kinds of places and for everything that you do inside,' Arun said as he clutched the paper ball and threw it at Dipu, 'that may sum up to a lot of money.'

Arun neatly folded the thin and dirty blanket, torn in different spots and placed it under his pillow. They had always lived on lanes, a different lane every year with their maternal aunt, who collected waste bits of paper from garbage bins and made money by selling them. Aunt Reba always said, 'you should leave your lane before they disown you...that saves the little dignity left in each of us.' They changed lanes usually after the tough days of monsoons were over, just before the onset of autumn, the festive seasons.

'Please Arun,' Dipu took Arun's hands and squeezed, 'Don't say that you won't. It's only for a day and we will earn money.'

'Will they let us go inside?'

'We'll pay them. That's all they need.' They looked at each other. Their eyes twinkled, gleaming with excitement, and they smiled.

Without wasting any time, as the sun moved away from the horizon, Arun and Dipu began to work harder. They washed more cars, cleaned more streets and earned more money by the time it was noon. They sat down under a bus stand. They counted their earnings by separating the different denominations of coins, exactly the way Aunt Reba taught them one day and said in her cracked voice, 'Kids! This is the most important learning of life – to count every penny earned, to earn every penny you count, and to make every penny you earn count.' They were sweating from exertion, but smugly pleased with the result of their hard work.

Dipu carefully separated the entry fee from the rest of their earnings while Arun joined the entry queue that stretched up to the next lane. They were now only a few steps away from their dreamland, too happy to realise the indifference of the world towards them. The parents and kids waiting in the queue maintained a careful distance from both of them. The line kept moving and they reached the ticket counter. A large, dark bearded man was seated at the table by the window as he called Arun. Arun bought two tickets from him.

At the entrance, the security guard wore a friendly countenance. He was a middle-aged stout and weasel-faced man. He smiled at all children and wished them warmly. When he saw Dipu and Arun, his face changed its colour, he barely looked up to greet them. He scanned them with a shrewd eye of suspicion, scrutinizing them from head to toe. He inspected the tickets carefully.

The gate opened to their world of fancy dreams.

'What should this note say?' Arun asked, pointing at huge board read in red, "HEARTY WELCOME TO YOU".

'That must, as usual, mean that we must pay money for everything we do inside. All they need is money and we've got enough!'

There were people dressed like clowns and animals moving all around to amuse the visitors and children posing for a photograph with them. A variety of rides filled the park at regular intervals... the Dragon Flight, Boat Ride, Jumping Mouse. Arun and Dipu ran around to see their dream being transformed into truth. As they walked, Dipu's attention was drawn at once by the enormous metal cage, skillfully made to fit the curve of the wall from floor to ceiling, filled with scores of tiny birds: green, blue, yellow and red. Drawing nearer, their eyes were startled to see them in a background of velvet green, darting among the artificial leaves of oak and chestnut. The cheerful conversing birds moved happily about their business.

They saw a flight of stone steps and climbed up to the top. There was a large room, round and rich with paintings hung against the sloping walls. It was luxuriously crowded with well born kids and their parents. The room was warmly lit by a fire to give the ambience of a castle. Their eyes gradually adapted to the dwindling light.

'Look, I'm a king,' Dipu cried, stepping on a small boulder near one of the walls.

'And I'm the king's brother!'

They laughed on their way down and came under the open sky once again. It was blinding with light.

'Look there at that thing!' Arun cried, pointing towards the Toy Train. Its deep green colour merged with the green of the trees as the serpent ran out of sight.

'It's so tiny!'

'It looked like a little serpent.'

'And children playing inside its tummy,' Dipu suggested, rubbing his hands on his chin.

'This train was so different from those we had seen last year when we lived in that narrow pathway near the station.'

'Hey Arun! The next ride will be ours! Let's get the tickets.'

The serpent arrived at the station for new prey for its next ride. Arun and Dipu hurried up and ran inside the train to get a window seat. The train regained its speed and they hung their heads almost on the edge of the window, closing their eyes and again opening them, delighted that their dreams were getting real. They sang, laughed and shouted as the train moved through the greenery. They were lost in their dreams. They dreamt of the sweet might-have-beens of life and stuck their eyes outside the window to feel and enjoy every moment of the ride, without giving the slightest care that no one else shared seats with them.

They walked around the cemented floor for car rides. Arun looked at Dipu and smiled expectantly. The sun was now gradually moving towards the horizon. The cars were moving irregularly on the floor and the horns were honking every now and then.

'I can drive a lot better than them actually,'Arun said, 'I'm sure I can. These rich kids are so stupid. They can't even drive straight!'

'No Arun, not this one,' Dipu declared, 'We've got little money left with us. Let's spend it on better things here. Not cars.'

'But they're so colourful, it'll be so much fun! Besides, I've never driven a car,' Arun said and lowered his voice, 'only washed them and seen them move away.'

'These are tiny cars, Arun. One day we'll ride bigger ones than these. Cars with black glasses that'll go down smoothly like they do when we knock them.'

They reached the lake. It was beautiful and caught the reflection of the dawning sun perfectly. The lake was surrounded by equally spaced trees and orchards. At one point, the tempting boats stood still, offering rides. Arun and Dipu looked dreamily at the sky, seeing dragon ships in the air. They were easily tempted by the shining navy blue paint on the boat that was called The Blue Whale and bought the tickets from a small boy, with a shock of glossy hair, curled up in the depths of his chair, clearly sleepy as the day was nearing its end. They stepped on the boat and sat quietly, looking at the water, waiting for two more people to complete the ride. It seemed the day was tainted by dreams. But the story of indifference repeated itself. The visitors kept refusing to take rides with Arun and Dipu when they saw them sitting inside the boat, dirtying the seats with the dust from their clothes.

The Blue Whale kept waiting as it got rejected by everyone. The manager of the park, a short, tubby man with a clerical dog collar, reached the spot on being informed. He patiently listened to the matter and after a brief apology for his absence promised the visitors that he'd look into it.

He turned towards the boy, still looking sleepy. 'You idiot, good for nothing fellow! Which parent would let their child ride with street children with untidy hair and torn, dirty shirts? Who would willingly share a ride with these kinds of filthy people? Who would spend time with beggars?

He then turned and looked at Arun and Dipu. His neck made a faint creaking noise and he looked at them angrily. He pulled them by their collars out of the boat.

'You've trespassed into the park!' shouted the manager, 'You must've crossed the boundary walls. I won't leave you. You don't realise what loss you've made to my business!'

'Sir,' replied Dipu, as the Manager was still holding his collar, 'we've bought tickets. I can show them.'

'Shut up, will you?' the manager shouted at the top of his voice, 'How dare you argue with me? I will hand you over to the police.' Dipu hurriedly took the tickets out of his pocket and showed them to the Manager. The Manager's face was red in anger. He began to thrash Dipu, first with his hands and then with his leather boots and continued abusing him. Others watched without a word as Dipu moaned in pain.

'Sorry Sir,' Arun apologized and bend on his knees to cover Dipu with his hands, 'this will never happen again. Please leave him. We'll never enter the park again.' A heavily built guard was called to throw Arun and Dipu out of the Nicco Park, where a huge board read in red, "VISIT US AGAIN". That must be saying that by-lane kids aren't allowed, they thought. A broad grin of delighted relief spread across the manager's face.

They walked silently down the footpath. There wasn't a queue at the entry gate, suggesting that the day was over. Arun and Dipu did not talk to each other. Like a moth, in the empty ambience of darkness, yearns to get out of oblivion and obscurity and seeks life in the form of a ray of light from a flame, they kept walking till they were close enough to their flame which they could seek bliss from, against the world's ugly truth. They kept walking till they could see Aunt Reba with the paper balls, waiting for them.

13

Fire Truck

'Fire truck!' yelled five-year-old Shyam running barefoot, clad in a torn shirt and trousers. He scuttled along the cobbled stones of the narrow street. He slowed down as the fire truck disappeared behind the ancient banyan tree that had grown through the crevices of an old, dilapidated temple opposite the City Palace that was on the other side of the broad main road. He retraced his way back, his head low and chin touching the chest. He walked to where his mother sat nodding dreamily in the sunshine at the backyard of their small mud house.

'Ma!' shouted Shyam, 'The fire truck is gone!'

Mala woke up from her day dream with a start and raising her head, displayed a face that looked much older when compared to women of her age.

'I called out...so many times! Baba! Baba!' he continued, 'The truck didn't stop! When I grow up I too want to be a fireman like him. Then, we all will live together in a big house.'

Mala smiled at him. 'Come Babu, sit. Are you hungry?'

'No. First tell me, why didn't Baba stop to see me?'

'How do you know that he was Baba?' Mala's eyes softened in revelation.

'Because he was inside the fire truck. You'd told me that he is a fireman! Then it was him.'

Shyam walked with his little steps and sat down beside Mala.

He fixed his eyes upon the huge round dot on her forehead. It looked like the full moon. He laid his head on her lap and murmured slowly, 'I'm happy, Ma, I saw Dad. One day I will speak to him and ask him why he left us and never comes back. I will bring him home.'

His father had left Mala when Shyam was about a year old. Shyam grew up only listening to stories about his father from Mala, never meeting him in real life. Whenever there was a fire, or a fire truck would run down the main road, Shyam's heart would dart to see his father. Mala would slowly call him nearer and calm him down with stories of a fireman, a tall dark man with a thick, black moustache and curly hair, identical to Shyam in multiple ways.

✦

The moon was hidden behind the thin layer of clouds. The forest was in a deep slumber, veiled in silence, under the combination of moonlight and darkness. The boys advanced rapidly along the tapered, grassy road through the woods, breaking the silence of the deserted, shadowy place. The tree tops moved in silent protest against the light from the lamps they were carrying. The trunks bend down to have a last look at Mala's dead body.

The moon emerged from behind the clouds. Shyam, ten-years-old, looked up. Mala's face appeared on the moon. She smiled at him before the fire engulfed her and burned her into ashes. He wiped his face with his little hands. He had come with Rana Mama, Mala's brother and a couple of men he knew in the neighborhood. Mala's toe curved in the fire. Shyam turned to hug Rana Mama. He said nothing on the way back. He returned home with Rana Mama who was now responsible for his welfare.

At Mala's funeral, Shyam sat in the darkest corner of the huge darkened house of Rana Mama, a couple of kilometers away from the house where he lived with Mala. His face illustrated nothing of what he felt or thought. He sat with Mala's photo – the person who meant the most to him. Nobody else had mattered ever, both of them had built a separate world for themselves, which had no one else, and now he was left alone in it. Nobody else had ever been of help to them in bad times, no one else had ever mattered – neither neighbours nor uncles nor aunts – least of all Shyam's father, the fireman, who lived miles away with another woman. They had lived all the years on the two hundred rupees that Rana Mama used to send them every month.

The house was full of visitors – relatives, family friends and neighbours. Some had attempted to console him but had been thoroughly dampened by his stillness, his tearless countenance. The more thoughtful of them had maintained a distance. Dispersed words of sympathy moved back and forth as if they were flies in the air. It was now time for the meal. Shyam stared through the window at the huge buckets which served the khichri, the ones serving and those who were eating. He had been forgotten for the moment.

Shyam kept sitting in the same place till the visitors had left in twos and threes, and then he got up from the dark corner and went out in the lawn. The lawn was the most beautiful part of the house. The gardener was sitting near a bed of lilies, upset because of the damage done in the funeral arrangement. He looked up and asked if Shyam needed anything. Shyam shook his head and departed inside the house. He had not eaten anything since morning. His eyes were red, he had been crying all night and it seemed that no more tears were left to run down his cheeks. Rana Mama and his wife were the only members in their family. They lived with one servant, one cook and a gardener. Everyone was tired after the day got over, ready for a slumber after a substantial meal.

Shyam slipped out of the house through the back door and made his way through a narrow gap in a thicket of marigold flowers into a lane. He kept walking till he reached the main road. It was the same road he had taken with Mala in the evening to buy groceries. It was the same road he would run like crazy after fire trucks to see his father. He reached the old banyan tree. The temple gate stood open but Shyam leant against its old stone wall and stared at the kids of his age who had come to pray with their parents.

Shyam closed his eyes. He felt a tender hand moving over his head. For a moment Shyam thought that Mala was beside him and they were on one of the evening walks together. Instinctively, he extended his hand, hoping for Mala's warm and comforting touch. Shyam opened his eyes. There was nothing, no one. He caught a blurry vision through his wet eyes of the temple priest. He was an old man in saffron dhoti. His eyes had grown small with age. His grey beard touched his chest.

'Why are you sitting here alone, child?' he asked.

'I'm hungry. I lost my mother. She died. May I get some food?'

'God has need of your mother,' he said. Shyam had heard these words of consolation throughout the day.

'Has your God, in a similar way, laid claim to all these men, women and kids who come to pray? Why my mother? I've got no one.'

'Says who? You stay here with me...with the little kids of your age who have no one. What's your name, child?'

'My name is Shyam. My mother called me Babu. Will I get food?'

Shyam walked inside the temple. At the end of the building, there was a big hall. Little girls and boys were playing. Shyam did not know whether to go forward or not. He was a little afraid. He looked behind. The air was getting cold. The road stretched outside the temple, behind him, empty, bathed in mist.

'The strongest man,' the priest said, 'is he who stands strong even when he's alone. And you aren't alone. Look there. There are so many like you.' He held Shyam's hands and called out, 'Prem Lal!'

'Yes *Swamiji*, 'Prem Lal appeared. He was a middle aged man in his early forties. He wore a saffron dhoti and kept his torso bare like Swamiji, the priest.

'This is Prem Lal. He has served the temple for thirty years. He had come to this temple when he was your age. He will show you your room.'

Prem Lal took out his hand to hold Shyam's. Shyam clenched his fists. He put them deep inside his pocket. In my world, Shyam thought, my mother is no longer here with me...how will I live alone...I need to look for my father...my world will soon have my father and me, no one else.

He followed Prem to the outhouse where the kids put their belongings. The outhouse was old and it was right beside the pond. It looked like a ruin from the outside, but from inside it was cool and comfortable.

Everyday Prem Lal opened the temple gate, cleaned the old, dried, crumpled flowers and leaves, watered the trees and helped Swamiji during the puja. The kids were also given their share of work – to help in cooking, to wash clothes, to look after the garden, to attend to the temple visitors. Shyam had to look after the garden – the roses, lilies, marigolds, sunflowers. Sometimes he thought about Rana Mama and wondered if they had bothered looking for him. It was good for them I came here, he thought.

He made friends but preserved his personal space. He knew he had to meet his father some day and complete his world. Till then he needed food to sustain himself and a place to live.

Fifteen years later the banyan tree still stood opposite the City Palace...the palace where the royals lived. The palace from a distance looked entirely made of ice, when observed closely it appeared to be built of white marble. The place was unbelievably, almost eerily quiet. Then the buzz started. A man went running up the temple stairs, past the banyan tree. He was shouting at the top of his voice – I sense danger, the fire-breaker will be here soon, everyone is saying the same in the marketplace.

Fear struck the place. People began to run and jostle around the temple. Swamiji and Prem Lal managed to push their way through the crowd to the main road. They could barely see much beyond the cloud of dust that hung over the road, created by the racing feet. Men and women were running in every direction, blindly pushing away almost everything that came their way, colliding against each other.

Swamiji and Prem Lal were pushed along the road in the direction of the palace. The people in front of them got scattered. They parted pushing along the sides of the road. Soon they were in the first rank of the crowd.

The air was suffocating. There was a lot of dark smoke that covered the sky. There was a familiar smell of something burning. The crowd's initial apprehension had melted away by then. Words started flowing in the air – who is the fire-breaker – I've heard he is not an Indian – This is the sixth time he has done this – what a jerk – why doesn't he come in front – what does he want?

Shyam, the notorious fire-breaker, had done it again. The City Palace was put on flames; Shyam had destroyed the castle. He darted to the side of the road and pushed himself against the wall. His once yellow T-shirt was tucked clumsily inside his torn trousers.

Soon the fire trucks arrived at the palace gate. The white marble stones had almost turned black with fire and smoke. Shyam rubbed his eyes and tried to look closely at the fire brigade. Why do they all look the same, he thought, how many such palaces do I need to set fire to in order to meet my father.

Almost a hundred men from the fire crew were fighting against the blaze. Shyam looked at the sky. Mala appeared between the clouds with the red dot on her forehead. Shyam closed his eyes. A tall man with curly hair and thick moustache walked out of the fire truck. He lived the moment for as long as he could.

14

Breaking Glass

Pssssta. I rushed to the kitchen after I heard the loud smash of breaking glass. Warmth was emanating from the hot, lemon scented chicken soup, with grey steam rising steadily to the low ceiling. To the right stood the white, bulky refrigerator that was always one of the first things that meet the eye.

'Wow! What was that? It was loud,' I exclaimed.

'Stop, stop! Be careful! There's glass there on the floor.' I looked down. The glass bottle lay in pieces near the lining of the refrigerator. It was messy and at a closer inspection revealed splatters of tomato sauce on the refrigerator door as well.

'How did this happen? I was just about to step on it! May I help?'

'I was looking for black pepper, got a bit unmindful and the sauce bottle fell off the shelf and now in pieces. God, I should've been more careful,' my mother said, 'I'll take care of it. I hope you aren't going out now.'

'Actually I was. I was taking Oreo for a walk outside. It's nice, sunny. Have a look from the window.'

Oreo was my best friend. He's a little puppy I had brought home some ten months back. He had white and black fur. I found him next to a garbage bin one evening when it was raining very hard, on my way from school. There was wind all the while it rained and I struggled to keep my umbrella straight. I heard a shrill noise. It was coming from the garbage bin by the pavement. The noise was a little thicker than a rat's squeak. I looked around.

The sky had a strange pinkish colour with a tinge of orange. The wind was rising. In the eerie light beneath the clouds, even the thoroughly modern houses along the road looked as antique and reddish as the Jorasanko Thakurbari that stood miles away. There was a tiny puppy at a corner. His fur was drenched in the rain water and he looked pinkish in the quirky colours of the sky. He was shivering in the cold wind. He was really tiny, about the size of my palm, probably two to three weeks old and could barely open his eyes. I went near him. The puppy was breathing very fast. He was weak and I brought him home. I named him Oreo. I did not want to burden him with pretentious names. I seriously considered Brownie or Chewie, Barney or Fuzzy. In the end I went with Oreo – it seemed to be a flawless and comical name for the cute, little, black and white, and funny dog that he was.

In the first few days, Oreo slept inside my blanket on my bed with a heating pad. Gradually, he could open his eyes wider but still depended a lot on me to help him stay warm and eat. Oreo was getting milk and bread once in every eight hours. The toughest challenge was to stimulate elimination. After meals, my mother rubbed a warm, wet cotton ball on his lower stomach. This made him eliminate following which my mother gently wiped away the waste. He was getting bigger and healthier under my attention. I tried to mimic his mother all the time. He was a scared, tiny dog, didn't run much and never bit people.

Bit by bit, he became my brother, my son and most significantly, we became friends. I got accustomed to his moves. He put one ear down and kept one up when he would be thinking, both ears down when he had done something wrong and bark every time I put on my cap because he knew we were going for a walk. He could run at an incredible speed. I usually did not chain him, I did not like the idea of leashing a dog, except when I walked him in the evening. Besides, he was a good dog. Oreo always waited at the gate for me when I returned from school. He would run towards me, his tail waving to and fro behind him.

'Ah! Don't go out just now. Didn't you see the glass bottle? It's not a good sign,' my mother said. Distractions, such as a loud splash of water gushing out of the faucet on the stainless steel plates, were common from the kitchen. But noise of glass breaking always brought a look of hopelessness on my mother's face. She had a strong belief that such unfortunate events were a bad omen. My mother wasn't very superstitious but she sturdily held to this one since my grandmother died in her sleep, the afternoon she dropped a glass water jug.

Meanwhile, Oreo returned to his couch where he was napping, sleeping on his back. He looked like he was smiling.

'I won't go far, I promise. He needs some air. C'mon Oreo, wake up! You lazy doggy!' I lied. It was I who needed air. I was bored.

Oreo ran out of the couch towards the store room. I watched his lean, muscular legs lurch violently forward as he tried to gain speed on the polished floor. He was an attention grabber I'd known for years. He just loved it. I hated it, though at times I found it adorable.

I followed him. There was a pile of newspapers, stacked near the door. I called out. A couple of tiny ears and little eyes peeped out of the pile to see if anybody was mad. A bit of dust had rubbed off on the white hair on his nose.

I walked down the lane with Oreo. Children on the rooftops were clutching spools of kite string and shouting. The desperate flutter of kites and young voices filled the air that moved the leaves of the trees by the footpath slowly.

Oreo was moving sluggishly that day. He is actually being unusual, I thought to myself. The road was empty. It usually was and sometimes we didn't see a car for many hours. There was no one except a small group of boys playing cricket. It was almost 5:30 in the evening.

I had always been an introvert, I loved being by myself. I didn't have too many friends, not because I was unfriendly...I enjoyed the calmness that solitude brings with itself. Often I had long thoughts about this. Lately, I discovered that it was only Oreo I loved to be with. It was only he who never made me wish I was invisible. I thought my reclusive nature, however, had made me a good thinker. May be I was wrong but this gave me a good feeling.

Those boys playing cricket were all of my age. I should talk to them someday, we all live in the same lane, I thought...but what if they don't talk to me...that'll not look good. These unsettling thoughts led to other thoughts. I don't belong to them...there is no ownership, no relationship without belonging. I sat down on the empty bench. I took Oreo in my arms. He started licking my face. He always did whenever he understood I was sad or something was bothering me.

Oreo suddenly raised his ears. A cluster of people came running towards us. A month back Oreo and I were sitting on the same bench...with similar unsettling thoughts running in my mind. A bunch of people came running towards us. Seeing the crowd, Oreo got so excited that he started running with them and the leash slipped from my hand. I called him back but he did not look back for once. Oreo never looked back when he would run. I had noticed this a number of times. I ran after him. I learnt that it was a marathon for cancer patients. I was a bad runner and the last to complete it but Oreo was ahead of everyone. He had raised twenty thousand rupees for the cancer centre that day. He appeared in the newspapers and news channels on the TV the next day. Oreo made me enormously proud that day. It occurred to me then that I should make a fan page for him on Facebook. I built a page for him and it all started with a joke and I thought it was a crazy thing to do. Oreo made few dog friends through it and that made me realise that there were so many crazy people out there. Gradually, Oreo had over two thousand "likes" in only a month, way more than the number of friends I had in my friend list. I think I was becoming a little green-eyed.

I turned towards Oreo. He had twinkles in his large, brown eyes and they lit up in excitement. I hugged him and this time we simply watched the crowd run.

A *puchka-wala* was pushing his van by the road. He stopped towards the end of the lane. We watched him ringing the little bell he always carried. Gradually, I noticed a small crowd of children and their mothers forming near the van. It has been quite a while since I had last had those fried puff pastry balls filled with mashed potato, spiced water and tamarind juice. I feel having them is an intimate way of enjoying Kolkata, the city of joy, mixing with its people, engaging in its aristocracy.

Oreo was standing on his hind legs and was using his front paws to lean on the bench. The next moment he was on the ground. My eyes were stuck at Oreo's awkward and uncoordinated puppy walk on the lane. A strong puff of wind ran across my face. It moved the trees violently and I felt dust inside my eyes. I let go of the leash and rubbed my eyes with my hands, just before the cricket ball with which the boys were playing reached the other end of the road. I heard the metal at the end of the leash as it made a scratching sound on the road. I saw Oreo running after the ball. I called him but like always, he never looked back. I ran after him and watched him cross the road. A huge truck moved fast across my eyes. I thought I had just avoided death. There was a sound of a popped tyre. Oreo made a whimpering cry.

I watched my dog get run over by the truck. The sound of breaking glass kept ringing in my ears as I sat on the side of the road holding him and crying. The wind was blowing hard and it was cold. The bright sky turned to a familiar pinkish shade. I ran towards him on the other end of the road. Oreo was lying near a garbage bin on the pavement. At first I thought he had fractured a leg, but soon he started vomiting blood. I looked around helplessly, desperately trying to keep him awake. The boys ran towards us as I sat with Oreo, unable to move.

'Call a cab,' one of them suggested.

'I doubt if we'll make it,' said another. I glanced up. 'Look at his eyes,' he continued, 'They're turning bloodshot!'

'You're so irresponsible, dude.'

'You're like this since you were small. You didn't change even this much. It's a shame!'

'It's your fault. Completely.'

'How will you ever come out of the guilt? Are you even guilty?'

'If you didn't know how to take care of a dog why did you bring it alone then? Why did you take its commitment in the first place?'

'Why did you let go of the leash! This dog will never forgive you.'

The words gradually faded in the air. I stared at Oreo for a moment. He was stunningly beautiful and despite his hard life before he came to me he was such a trusting friend. He called me with his weak voice. I saw his eyes as he passed away in my arms and just before he died, I moved my hand slowly over his head and he licked the tears off my face.

15

Little Crayons at the Back Gate

The lanes of Mumbai were glowing on the winter morning. The pani puri stalls lined themselves by the footpath. The cars got more impatient with every passing minute as they moved in the dirty air. The dusty roads got filthier every hour. Gradually, the shopkeepers banged their shutters open. As the sun got hotter, vada pav and tea proved again to be an integral part of the city.

'What an odd place to sleep,' a passer by screamed, 'We don't have any place to even walk.'

Raju and her elder sister, Deepali opened their eyes. A thin quilt was tucked clumsily under their chin. They lived on the footpath, under the shade of an oak tree in their small one room home made out of large plastic sheets, with their mother. Their mother worked hard all day and usually left home while the two of them were still sleeping.

'Deepali,' said Raju, rubbing his eyes, 'it's morning, wake up' Deepali yawned loudly and kept her eyes closed against the glare of the sun. She took a stone that was lying beside her and rolled it repeatedly. She eased herself and held on to her head to prevent it from rolling down on the pillow and bouncing on the ground. Raju sat down and rubbed his eyes.

'Today is Sunday, so no school,' Raju said sleepily, 'it'll be so boring.'

'Why don't we do something interesting then? I'll tell you, I'd this idea last night.'

'Like swimming in that lake near the next lane? Remember? It was so much fun the last time we did it!'

'We'll make Rishabh Bhaiya a gift,' said Deepali as she rolled up the blanket, shaking her head in excitement. The sun lit her hair with flames of gold and copper.

'But why?' He looked at her quizzically.

'Raju...Rishabh Bhaiya tries so hard to teach us the LMNOPs in school...'

'And counting 123.'

'He loves us so much.' They looked at each other and smiled on the day dream tainted morning.

'But what should we give him? We can't buy him gifts. I don't have money, do you?'

'Remember what Bhaiya said on the first day in school, Raju?'

'To wish each other good morning? Oh, I forgot. Good Morning!'

'No silly! He said that in this world no one is rich or poor. We all are gifted! So Raju, when we all are gifted, can we not gift him?'

'I can't understand...what do you mean?' Raju was confused. He looked at Deepali as she scratched her once white sweater.

Deepali took out a white paper and a small wooden box from her withered school bag with broken zip that hung on a loose string. She carefully unpinned the rusted safety pin.

'So you see this box, Raju? I found it lying near the City School back gate.'

'So why did you bring it with you?'

'I was on my way back, the other day, when mother asked me to get some onions. I saw a girl in school clothes, walking out of the gates. She took this box out of her bag and threw it on the road. I noticed and picked it up quickly and ran.'

'Didn't she see you? The guards, didn't they spot you picking it up? They could've caught you. They would've scolded you. Mother would've been so angry.'

'I don't know. But I really doubt if they would care about little things as these. Big people have bigger things to worry about.'

'What's inside?'

'Very small pieces of crayons. Let's make a painting for Bhaiya.'

'Don't you think we must give this to the guards of the school?'

'I doubt if we should. I was thinking the same. But children in the school have better bigger newer crayons. We can have the smaller used ones.'

'So we'll paint on this paper. What shall we make?'

Deepali rolled her eyes around the place and said, 'First, I need a table...which we don't have here. I need something hard to rest this paper on.'

'The ground is dirty. The white paper will turn brown. And then the background of the painting will be brownish,' Raju put his tiny thumb inside his mouth and giggled.

'Do you see that bike on the other end of the road, there, near the photocopy shop, beside the brick wall?'

'There are two of them, one and two, a red and a black bike.'

'No. The black bike, it is there for a very long time. The red bike has just come, I didn't see it since morning. I think the black one will make a very good table.'

They clutched each other's fingers and quickly crossed the road. Deepali carefully opened her notebook and placed it on the bike seat. Then she positioned the paper on it.

'What do you want to make?' Deepali asked.

'I can't draw...will you make a jumping mouse for me, one with big eyes and that which looks mischievous?'

'Sounds very amusing. I'll make a jumping, big eyed, mischievous mouse and a colourful, smiling crow.'

'But crows are black and they don't smile.'

'But I've got crayons which will give it colours and I'll make it smile.'

'So how will you colour the mouse?'

'Colour it blue?'

'No, it will look like a dead mouse then, killed by a naughty cat.'

'Then maybe we can have a naughty cat beside it as well!'

Deepali used shades of blue, green, orange, red...they laughed all the way down the beautiful picturesque moment.

'The mouse!' Raju shouted.

'What's with the mouse? Does it look like you wanted it to be or is it funny?'

'No! It looks absolutely like the movie Bhaiya showed us last day in school.'

'Really? It looks like Jerry! But I don't think the crow came out very well. I believe my crow looks more like a sparrow, no, a parrot!'

'Do you think Rishabh Bhaiya will be angry that this crow isn't accurately like a crow?'

'I don't know. I haven't ever imagined an angry Bhaiya. He has always been very nice and jolly with us. I don't know if he gets angry.'

All of a sudden, a pair of hands in black leather jacket hugged both of them from behind, 'So what are my little friends up to this morning on my bike?' Raju and Deepali turned around.

'Rishabh Bhaiya!' they shouted. Rishabh Bhaiya was standing with his arms surrounding them. The chiseled lines of his face, his dark hair, the level brows and wide brown eyes stood against the sun.

'Bhaiya, do you get angry?' Raju asked.

'Will you get angry? The crow doesn't appear like a crow, I wanted to make it colourful but it ended up like something else,' Deepali said.

Rishabh Bhaiya slowly turned aside to look at the painting. His deep scarlet coat had golden buttons that gleamed intensely. An expression of mingled happiness and curiosity showed on his striking dark face. 'Yes I do get angry at times. And when I do, it's bad. But a crow can always look like something else if you want it that way, Deepali. The crayons are in your hands and you're absolutely free to do anything with it...you're in complete control of the way you want things to be! Like, I would love to call it Deepali's crow which looks like this. Now no one in this world would question why Deepali's crow is so strange! So is this beautiful drawing for me, is it?'

'Yes, Bhaiya it's for you! It's a gift!' Raju said.

'I've never had a gorgeous gift as this one, kids! I'm so glad that you've had your Bhaiya in your minds when you made this.'

'Bhaiya, is this your bike?' Raju asked.

'No, my friend's. I needed a bike so my friend helped me. Like you should always help your friends.'

'What's this written on your bike, here, down, in white? I can see a two and a zero and a zero,' Raju said.

'That makes a two hundred, Raju. We'll learn all that very soon. I'm tremendously pleased today. You should in fact look at numbers and words you see here and there and try to read them.

This is a very good habit and will make you learn faster. Raju, Deepali...come along!'

'Where?' Raju asked, 'To school? We have no school today.'

'True, I wish there was and I could show this good-looking painting to your friends and other teachers. But for now, it's time for some fun.'

They walked towards a little gift shop that stood nearby. Rishabh Bhaiya pushed the glass door, laughing and joking with them, and stood back to let them go first up the narrow and dark front steps.

'Bhaiya,' Deepali whispered, 'what if they scold us and turn us out!'

Rishabh Bhaiya looked into Deepali's eyes and said, 'Why should they...that won't.'

The shop looked welcoming. It was equipped with long flowing curtains on the enormous windows, but still providing a great deal more light than had been available in the fashionably gloomy steps, hooks on the walls carrying banners of discounts, and open shelves carrying stationary items. The air was thick with the delicious, sweet scent of the room freshener. A long counter ran along the side, displaying a remarkable assortment of toys, story books and pencils. Raju and Deepali looked around the gorgeously festooned place, the rivetingly fascinating toys that they had never seen before. Everything was immaculately clean.

A short, middle-aged serving woman was sitting at the counter. Rishabh Bhaiya picked up a huge box of crayons from the shelves at the extreme end of the shop. After a small conversation with the woman he paid for the box and left the shop with both of them.

'For us!' they cried.

'Yes! My return gift for both of you.'

'But this is a very big box,' Deepali insisted, 'It must be having a lot of crayons inside. What will we do with so many?'

'Paint and paint more. Think how you can put these crayons to their best use. I'm so proud of you. See you two in school tomorrow!'

Rishabh Bhaiya got on his bike and sped away in the busy highway. The two of them strolled back towards the other end of the street.

'What will we do with this new box of crayons? We have one already,' Raju said and turned towards Deepali.

'Yes. This is so new and we've never had new things.'

'Smell it. I think I like the smell of new stuff.'

'Don't. We mustn't be used to new things. Mother says that it's a wrong habit to be used to something that doesn't last forever.'

'But doesn't she say that when she brings us good food? Those potato flakes in blue and green packets.'

'But I know it applies to everything else in life and besides, she also says we must make the best use of whatever little we have. Rishabh Bhaiya also said that we must put these crayons to their best use. We already have the smaller ones and there is so much colour still remaining in those.'

'So should we...'

'I was wondering if we should go back to the City School and give it to the guards. And when these crayons become as little as the ones I brought, we can always bring them home.'

'What if they don't give you when they're small?'

'Don't worry, Raju...they'll always be lying near the back gate of the school.'

The glossy paper that covered the box reflected the sunlight, throwing the sun's brilliance back. Their small plastic paper home looked receiving, calling them nearer. The sun glowed over them, throwing a miniature shadow on the road. Warm air was accompanying the heating of the day and the fluttering of leaves made multiple shadows dancing on the footpath. They could imagine fairies in the sky, dancing with the air, throwing their shadows near their plastic home.

16

The Last Kiss

Charu cleaned up the dinner table and was walking towards her bedroom. She turned the dim lights on. The yellow light beautifully reflected the red carpet, on the stairs, onto the marble floor. She stopped to look at the huge mirror on the wall and took out the red bindi from her forehead and stuck it on the mirror. She combed her hair. It was long and curly and black. She adjusted her sari and was walking towards the store room to look for a discarded cloth, a rag for the next day's dusting. She pushed open the wooden latch and stepped inside a shabby room woven of dust and filth. She slowly closed the door behind her.

Charu bent down, looking for the rag, unmindful of the dust veiling the floor. The anklets stopped clinging when her eyes fell on a yellow postcard. It was old and wrinkled, lying under a stack of old newspapers, half hidden in their shadows, beside the waste paper basket at the nearest corner. She pulled it out.

The postcard was covered with dust. Charu cleaned it with her hands. The dust made her cough. It was her mother's letter... the last that her mother wrote to Charu, seven years back. Charu sat down on the floor and began to read it in her mind.

'Trust this finds you in good health Charu. How is London this winter? Is it colder this year?'

She looked around, unmindfully. She found a once yellow piece of cloth lying beside where she was sitting. How many times she had helped her mother find bits of old cloth. She smiled as she remembered the fun they had trying to guess the original outfits that the piece of cloth belonged to...often they would be Charu's old frocks that she wore when she was little. She missed those days dearly. She continued to read the letter.

'It has been years since your father passed away. Strange that time flies really soon. It was just last night that I was thinking about you, how you grew up in front of my and your father's eyes, barely letting anyone realise.'

Charu smiled as she went on. The big pendulum wall clock moved to and fro eleven times.

'Remember the sweets I used to make for Bijoya? Narkel narus? This year I was making them for the neighborhood kids. They are very fond of those. I forgot to add camphor, I realised later. I'm getting forgetful these days...I'm aging fast it seems.'

The narrow muddy roads with ponds on either side...Charu could almost feel the innocent smell all the way from her home, where she grew up. The fresh grass, the morning dewdrops on the leaves, the hens...everything called her nearer, where the blue sky lined the wide fields perfectly, where the beautiful white pigeons moved freely in the sky. Charu would stare at them, at the white of the birds and the blue of the sky merging entirely with each other.

On Bijoya Dashami celebrations, her mother woke up very early in the morning when the sun was yet to break open the night sky. The dewdrops would shine on the lotus petals in the pond and the breeze would gently carry the smell from the kitchen when she would grate the coconut for the *narkel narus*, the ball shaped coconut confection made of condensed milk, coconut and sugar.

Charu looked at the cloth she found. It was still lying on the floor beside her. This bit of once yellow cloth with green polka dots was from her yellow skirt. She went back to the summer mid-morning, the year she turned nineteen. She was hungry since she had kept a fast for the Dashami Puja. Her eyes fell on the steel plates of narkel narus that her mother had kept on the table outside the kitchen. She walked slowly towards them, careful that she made no noise. She did not think anyone would come near the tiny room outside the kitchen where the table was. A steep staircase near the kitchen ran up to the roof. She picked up a couple of narkel narus and smelled them.

'Don't touch them, Charu,' her mother shouted. She was climbing down the stairs. Charu looked helplessly around her as if to look for a partner in her crime. But there was none.

> *'Today morning I came across a very old photograph. Your father and I were sitting at our coffee table. We both must had been in our 20s. Scores of memories ran down my mind. Just then I happened to notice something which I didn't see before. On the back side of the photograph in your father's handwriting I read: In this time we were infinite. And suddenly I realised that he has left us, suddenly I felt so alone in this big house and all of a sudden a shiver ran down my spine. All that I do now is writing down these little snippets of my rather long life which has formed a king size memory till date. Often, I stare at the walls…I can almost see you, the little Charu from years back, how you would hold the walls and struggle to walk with your tiny steps moving irregularly. Seems like it was yesterday. Now even the walls, I believe,*

miss your touch with those little fingers. And when I'm tired of writing my diary, I make narkel narus for the kids. These seem like inseparable parts of my living now.'

Charu looked at her hands, they were bigger...her fingers were longer...the veins showed up so green and clear.

'I know you get angry when I talk about it, but let's face it. Since I'm aging fast I don't expect much from life. It can be my turn any day. Do go through the diary I've been writing in the past few days. You will get to learn a good detail about those days when you were small and your father and I would spend long hours to decide how to bring you up. I keep it inside the brown cupboard, the wooden one, after I have finished writing. The next time you visit India, take it with you. I may or may not be there.'

Charu looked away. She had brought her mother's diary to London the last time she went home. Her mother had passed away by then. Scores of emotions would overcast her all day long whenever she would read her mother's diary.

'Where are you going?' Bijit had asked Charu as she swung her leg out of the bed the morning after she finished reading the diary.

'I've got to try and do something for Mother. I must,' she replied, sitting on the side of the soft and cozy bed, she bounced gently up and down, creating slight rhythmic motion.

Charu looked at his confused face. 'Bijit, I had no idea that she was such a good writer,' she continued, 'She presented almost her whole life in this diary. It's her memoir. I've learnt so many things I hadn't known before.'

She looked at the floor and in a softened voice said, 'I was thinking of the possibilities, maybe a publisher.' She looked up and rolled her eyes, sensing an outburst, but Bijit smiled kindly and encouraged her, saying that she should. Charu glanced through the window where the elm trees were lashing to and fro. The air made a loose shutter banging somewhere on the other end of the road and that reminded her that she should close their window. She walked across the room and stood near the window.

'It seems a difficult task here in London though I'm going to try my best,' she said.

'What new things did you learn about her?'

'Bijit, my mother grew up when India wasn't a free country and that's how she showed how she despised the British. She wrote little poems, patriotic ones, in between the paragraphs. And then very vivid details about how she grew up, her play mates, the dolls she played with. And then the little family disputes with her uncle and eventually getting married to my father...the lonely days she spent in the initial years of marriage when my father was working in Chandigarh and the tough days with my grandmother, her mother-in-law, she seemed to be very strict, a typical perfectionist. I kind of knew that when I was small, but then she passed away when I was still very little. Gradually she learnt to be a disciplinarian herself. And then I was born, my father still away from all of us. She quoted the letters that they exchanged, how they loved and missed each other, how they'd planned to bring me up, the values of morality...'

'But who do you thing will be interested in all that account,' Bijit laughed a bit sheepishly and followed her across the room, still talking, 'But tell me, she did mention me somewhere, didn't she?'

'She did,' Charu agreed settling herself on the dressing table seat, 'I've always known that she was very fond of you and I'm sure that even you know that. She wasn't very happy that we had to live in London.'

'She could've always chosen to live with us here in London had she wished to. I suggested that so many times.'

'You may have suggested that she should start living here. I could have insisted that I missed her and she would definitely have come here. But that would've been really unfair to her. After my father passed away, I'd known my mother to hold onto the memories she had with him. And then I too started living away from her after marriage. What I've always thought was probably all this must've really made her a little insecure about her life. But I realised she had the greatest of all companions, her memories and the diary.'

He had poured a glass of water for himself as she continued, 'She had more reasons for being resentful. She feared that we may not return to India and that she would die without seeing me for the last time. And that's what exactly happened, Bijit. And the last kiss that none of us could recall.'

'The last kiss? I don't know what you're talking about. It's getting late, go to sleep. We'll talk about publishers tomorrow.'

Charu had looked for publishing agents for many years. She had written to every large and small publishing house in London. She had given up when none of them responded positively.

Charu stood up as she reached the end of the letter.

'Another small thing I realised lately. It has been very long that I've kissed you, Charu. I cannot recall when I did the last time, not since you were a small girl I think. Had you been here I would have. Take care of your health. Love.'

Hot tears welled up. They threatened to fall down her cheek. She wished if she could turn back time, if she could stay near her mother, if Bijit never moved to London, if she could see her mother for few more years.

Her mother died a month after she wrote the letter. Charu thought back to the time when she last kissed her mother. She could not recall. She quickly kept the postcard aside and rushed to her little daughter who turned eight a month back. She was sleeping soundly, smiling in her dreams. Charu slowly entered the room and planted a kiss on her cheek. There was a tiny imprint of saliva but Charu didn't wipe it away. Charu looked at her for some time before she adjusted the blanket and walked towards the door.

A puff of air brought the autumnal hues of aspen leaves and the vivid smell of narkel narus from the distant land where she had spent her childhood observing the various shades of orange on the sky, land and under water. I will never let my nerves forget a last kiss to her, she thought as she closed the door behind her.

17

The All-Rounder

Like Rishi, my distant cousin, there are many among us who, given an opportunity, would be happy to leave India and go abroad. Given a chance, even I would have. But that was before I knew about financial intoxication. My friends might have thought that I am crazy. They still do. However, now I'm almost paranoid at the thought of going away and not coming back, leaving behind old parents in India. This was due to a transition that has taught me so much about life – the little joys that we tend to overlook. I think I shall always be obliged to Manohar Uncle for sharing the greatest knowledge of what he calls – the financial intoxication.

Towards the end of the monsoons, on a clear September day, I visited Manohar Uncle in Mumbai. I had applied for a job in a glass manufacturing company and I was staying with Manohar Uncle in his house while I went through the interview process. Manohar Uncle is forty-five-years-old and is the owner of a huge fortune. I've always regarded him as an influential businessman worth hundreds of millions and aspired to become like him.

Manohar Uncle is my father's distant cousin. He lived in a huge bungalow in the middle of the city. It looked new – very new – like it was built yesterday. It had huge windows complemented by bright flowery curtains. The house looked to me like a live, contemporary castle. The rooms were big, not too empty. The bungalow had an enormous iron gate with a design of growing tendrils that opened to the garden. Scarlet and saffron primroses, golden-headed clusters of defiant daffodils and lilies filled up a major part of the front and the side rows. On the other end, there was a huge shed which protected his cars.

I loved the stone path that led to the main door – punctuated with wild flowers at the end of every stone. At one of the bright corners, a cherry tree swayed in the winds – they moved gently with the air, calling me nearer. I recalled the cherry seed I had planted there when I was seven years old. The cherry tree is what reminds me of my village, everything else is highly posh.

It often gives me a fright to imagine living in this enormous house alone with a handful of servants like Manohar Uncle does. His son, five years elder to me, has settled in London. I don't think I remember much about Uncle's wife, she died when I was very small. I had been in this house for over two weeks now.

One evening, when I returned from the job interview, I saw Manohar Uncle, suited up, at the landing outside the kitchen door. He was tall, fair, had good teeth, black, deep-set eyes and was dressed smartly in business formals. He had a Mont Blanc pen placed inside his Armani suit pocket. I loved his Movado watch.

'Good evening, Tatai,' he said walking towards me. Patting my back he continued, 'How did the interview go, son?'

'Can't say really. They always seem satisfied with whatever I say and I guess they look satisfied always. God knows what's behind their smile. I think there should be another round of interview towards the end of the next week. Are you going somewhere?'

'We're going somewhere. Leave your bag here. The driver is taking the car out.'

We took our seat in the silver grey car, and cruised down the busy black velvet ribbon draped street.

'Where are we going, Uncle?'

'Nowhere! Sometimes I like going nowhere, a long drive and back.'

'Long drive!' I exclaimed. May be, I thought, this is a rich businessman's pastime. 'How often do you go for one?

'Not often. It gets boring without someone to talk to. Now that you're here, we may go once in few days.'

'But don't you often go out for parties with your friends and partners in business?'

'Tatai,' he said turning towards me, 'a person like me, who earns hugely and has a gigantic cash balance in the bank, sadly, doesn't have too many friends he can trust.' He turned to face the window.

'Uncle, you've made a commendable achievement. You're an inspiration, truly.'

Manohar Uncle looked at me and gave the most sarcastic smile I've ever seen coming from him. 'It looks good from where you stand, Tatai. At your age I, too, had big dreams. I wanted to become the richest, and the best.'

'What's wrong in aiming that high? I say, life's short, get as much as you can.'

'Ha...ha Son, I can see myself from my twenties in you. I used to think and say exactly the way you do now.'

'I don't understand. In one year, I suppose, by saving a little part of your earning you can create assets worth a lot more than what most people would be able to in, say, ten years.'

'Exactly, Tatai. This is what I'm suffering from...have been fighting against this financial, I would call it, intoxication.'

'What is financial intoxication?' I asked. I wasn't able to perceive most of what Manohar Uncle was saying. Perhaps, I thought, this was a rich man's virtual regret.

'There is no English word I know that describes my situation, so I call it financial intoxication, I suppose this is the closest. Tatai, I've, since many years now, had, or suffered from, a kind of belief, a feeling where I know that there is no perceivable shortage for the supply of money. Then I reached a stage in life where money was not significant because there was an ample supply of it.'

'That's what must have given you the stability, Uncle.'

'Stability, yes. Because even crores of rupees did not matter much because I always believed, as a matter of fact, the following year I would be earning a lot more.'

'That's cool!!! Nothing in life seemed unachievable, mustn't be so?'

'Plus, the power of my chair, my position. Add to that the fame, the popularity that comes from the network I'm a part of. I realised that I was at the pinnacle of success and that I could change lives because then, my views, my decisions were worth several hundreds of crores.'

'Why are you repenting all this? I sure would like to be like you some day!'

'Well, if you really love being alone, all by yourself, with few servants around...and end up your life in between the lifeless furniture and wealth of all kinds.'

'Why should financial intoxication do this to you? You'll die in the best city hospital...headlines bearing the news!'

'Tatai,' he said turning towards the window, his voice softened, 'I've lost your Aunt really early in our marriage. Anita was a very adorable person. More importantly, she was very emotional. She wanted my attention and time. All I was concerned about was owning all this – a big house, car, money – I devoted all my time to my business, professional success, social status and career. Do you know how she died? She committed suicide. And I know why she did it. It was because of me. Can you believe it, Tatai, I didn't get time even to mourn her death? This life gets to nowhere.' He spoke to me without turning from the window.

I looked at him. He didn't have tears in his eye but his face turned serious. I didn't know if it was apt to say anything at that moment.

I had always regarded myself as useless since at least half my life had been spent in idleness. My old school would not be proud of me, nor would the engineering college I've studied from, nor would my father.

'You spend most of your time sitting in the backyard, doing nothing,' my father scolded when I was eleven or twelve, 'what are you doing?'

'Nothing.'

'Are you thinking?'

'No, Baba.'

'Are you dreaming? What are you doing there? Why don't you use your time in better productive ways?'

I was born in a poor family. My father worked in our school. He was a clerk. Sitting in the backyard, apparently doing nothing, has always been my favorite form of inactivity. It was not until I was in class twelve that I realised I had to study and help my father run the house. It was then that I started aiming to become like Manohar Uncle. And now, seeing him in an utterly different light has shaken the foundation of my beliefs.

'What about, Rishi? Your son has made you so proud. He's doing so well in that country.'

'Rishi! Did you know he was a talented guy – apart from

studies he did exceptionally well in sports and music when he was in school. He had hockey practice sessions every morning and music classes in the evening.'

'Seems like he was born to win. Baba always gives his example – good in studies, sports, music – in everything he did.'

He smiled and turned towards me. 'You know Tatai, he was given the All-Rounder Prize in his last year in school. Yes!'

'He made you proud!'

'He makes me proud now. Back then I did not bother about his sports and music activities. Can you believe it, my son used to come home with invites for basketball matches and music concerts? I never found time for any of them. I don't think I had even held a proper gaze at the All-Rounder Prize. My business was this important to me. I feel terrible now when I think how the poor kid had lost his mother at such a little age, it must have been difficult for him. Had I been more thoughtful towards him, he wouldn't have left for London. He's left home because he hates living with his dad! This is what I've made out of my life. My business is my biggest enemy, had never imagined it to be.'

'Has he ever told you about this, his feelings for you, before leaving for London?'

'Had he ever talked to me I would've been so lucky. No, he seldom speaks to me. When he does, it's got to do something with money. I've lived all my life for money and this is exactly what I've got back in return.'

I looked at Manohar Uncle, he closed his eyes and was shaking his head sadly. I recalled my childhood at once. I loved to sing songs of Tagore as a child and I still do. My father was very fond of music, especially Indian Classical music. He had an impressive collection of records and cassettes. We travelled a great deal to the cities to listen to singers.

Financial intoxication, I thought, is indeed gorgeous, it gives you everything you wish for – but looking at Manohar Uncle I felt really bad. But I don't know why it made me smile. May be because my father is probably only worth half as much as Manohar Uncle's last pay check, but he made it to my music performances when I was small, even though I had never won an All-Rounder Prize.

Manohar Uncle continued to look outside the window. We did not speak during the rest of the drive. I was his companion in silence for a short time. By then I had decided to stay near my parents, always, no matter what.

18

The Fading Cloud

Earrings have always fascinated me. They give an elegant finish to the delicate curves and folds of the human ear. I've had this gold earring ever since what it seems like forever. I was only four years old when Thakuma, my father's mother had passed away. My mother tells me that this earring was given to me as one of her few last wishes. I've always wondered why it was me that she had chosen from a pool of granddaughters though I was glad that she did. Now that I think about it, the answer strikes me from a fading cloud of memories.

The earring, made of gold, has green stones studded on it and the filigree patterns give it the royal look it carries. The golden chains hanging from it finishes the work beautifully.

Thakuma was not the traditional grandmother. That's typically how my mother's mother was...grandmotherly, never short of spare change. I don't recall Thakuma giving me tight hugs or fussing over my health. I can't even remember talking to her for long hours nor listening to her childhood stories, neither did she even stuff me up with my favourite dishes. Thakuma wasn't a typical granny. But while she didn't stitch dresses for my dolls or teach how to sing, her superior personality and characteristic interests most definitely made a mark on my vulnerable mind.

Thakuma was known all her life as *Surobala* which means daughter of the Gods. She was born in Bangladesh which was in

India then. She came to live in Calcutta after she got married to my grandfather. She raised three sons and three daughters. I've seen very few aspects of Thakuma and I feel that I've missed a lot of her.

Thakuma was not like the typical fat and warm little grandmas. She was tall and petite. She had a long face with extremely sharp features. Her hollow cheeks, wheatish complexion, silvery grey hair teamed up with a straight posture could easily pass off as an outlandish and alluring royalty. Her eyeliner would often leave charcoal patches under her eyelashes. Her lips always had the red of the betel leaves. I remember her in a white sari with bright red border and that's the only image I've saved in my mind for Thakuma. With her glasses, drawing from a richly ornamented case, at the tip of her nose she practiced the role of a strict disciplinarian in the house. But the imprint left upon my mind by her form will never be eroded, particularly her curiously prominent, dull dark eyes and how she would read and smile, smile and read the novels of Tagore sitting in her high backed arm chair, as happy and complete as a grandmother could possibly feel.

I've seen more of Dadu, Thakuma's husband, who died when I was in the eighth standard and can remember a good deal about him. He wasn't really a family person. He was the headmaster of a local school and spent most of his time in his study room. He was a lost wonderer, a philosopher, a mathematics freak. I feel this could've been the reason behind Thakuma's upper hand in family matters and that her opinion was regarded as one of the greatest importance. She rarely smiled and possessed an inexpressible kind of manner which placed everyone under the persuasion that they are continually doing, thinking or telling something wrong. And this always made everyone around her greatly obliged whenever there was a convergence of an opinion with hers. She could easily assume a strict and powerful air. Her children, though they feared and never dared to argue her authority, also loved her dearly.

My father tells me that in her young age, she had to struggle a lot. In time, she came to have electric irons, washing machines and room heaters. But her life as a mother and wife did not begin like that. It was all hard work – washing, scrubbing, wooding and cleaning. I imagined her having blissful moments with the women in her neighborhood as she did that. I think she was proud, having endured her early poverty, perhaps even enjoyed it, given the kind of a persistent woman that she was.

Thakuma was a devout worshipper. She had a separate praying room where she kept the idols of Gods and she had a huge collection of them. She prayed twice a day – once after she took a bath in the morning and again just after the sun would drop behind the trees that lined the house. And every time she prayed she began with blowing the conch shell and ended by ringing the worship bell. I remember being a regular companion to Thakuma during the morning and evening prayers. I don't think that I was religious as a child. I believe I was tempted by the sweets that she offered to the Gods. She always said that there is a God in everyone and that washed away the guilt of such unethical temptation.

A couple of months before Thakuma's death we moved out of her house. My father, mother and I started living in another house in a place called Chittaranjan. My father was doing his internship from a hospital nearby and this made Thakuma a different person that I ever knew. I vividly remember that once, before she died, we visited her and on our way back we sneaked out of the house in the middle of the night. This was like a ten minutes secret mission...moving the luggage outside, calling the guards, seeing Thakuma before we left...it was fun! I understand now how badly that hurt her confidence.

I knew that Thakuma was insecure. Thakuma always thought that my father loved me more than he loved her. She gradually built up a sense of competition against me and I could sense this very early in my childhood. I recall how she would often tease me by saying, 'My Papa! My Papa!' I would cry and she would have a smile of satisfaction at the corner of her lips, dyed red by the betel leaves.

I remember once, after watching a violent horror movie, I abruptly asked her how she wanted to die. 'Like the sunset,' she'd replied. She was a woman of fervent and unwavering faith. A serious woman, Thakuma sometimes joked too. Once she said, 'I never really meant to live this long. I would have been quite satisfied to go before.' She had utterly no panic of death and was extremely keen to join her God.

Thakuma was a strong advocate of home-made remedies. Once I fell sick and she gave me all these remedies made by her special formulae with things like cinnamon tea. And when I was better she would visibly take pride and say, 'remedies work better, much better than any antibiotic' and so far I too believe her.

Thakuma had invited me once on a fruit picking expedition for a grand Lakshmi Puja with several other women in the neighborhood. I had accepted with alacrity since I was extremely eager to get out of the forbidding walls. Thakuma had a beautiful garden. I greatly enjoyed wandering through the cool breeze of spring morning, touching the damp leaves of the fruit and vegetable trees for the bright mangoes, smooth and pulp brinjals, and shiny green guavas, squeezing gently to judge their ripeness.

We were careful to pluck only the best. We dropped them into our baskets in juicy heaps.

'Will there be a lot of visitors today?' I asked Thakuma.

'More than last year, the more the visitors, the better goes the year.'

Visitors were already beginning to arrive at the house, most of whom I had never seen before. I kept a close eye on the comings and goings, and made a point of making frequent visits to the kitchen to smell the *Bhog*, the food for the Goddess. The yellowish brown containers used for making the Bhog were enormous in size and I often imagined eating inside them.

I don't remember any more about Thakuma except for the fact that she passed away soon after. She had a stroke. I can recall that day, like it was yesterday. The sun was glimmering, the birds were tweeting, the wind was breathing, but Thakuma was gone. I had seen how much my father had cried for her, perhaps more than anybody else cried on that day. Thakuma, I thought then, would've been happy to see how much my father missed her. Perhaps, few days before her death when she kept aside the earring for me, she realised that no one could take the position of a mother...a mother especially as uncommon as Thakuma. She is beautiful in my memories forever, since she died so young.

Though I've spent a very little part of my life in her house, no matter where I am or what I remember, my mind takes me back to that place, across trees and ponds and lakes. If I close my eyes now, I am there at the green wooden door, the summer sun blazing down on white rod fences and grills heavy with honeysuckle and creepers, a rebellion of creeping plants and little flowers dripping bees. Below them, along the grassy path to the door, there will be sweet peas and how I loved picking them and having them as much as my hands could hold. Every summer there were sweet peas, staked up against the fence. It was always comfortable and cool under the canopy of green that leads to the door. There were two huge oak trees and one mango shading the back windows. They smelled tempting in the summer months. At any time of the day, it was always shady inside the house. All the trees and the covered front veranda kept it from sunlight, making the backyard of the house the best spot for drying washed clothes. One thing that still hovers in my mind is the creepy feeling while going down the dark passage to the toilet. At the end of the passage there was a glass table with the electric iron, the telephone and little brass show pieces.

There would not be much sunlight, but there was always noise – of birds chirping, radio and people, her girlfriends from the neighborhood. They came in waves in the evening. They sang, laughed, talked about their husbands, complained about recent ailments and gossiped in the backyard. Thakuma would feed them tea. She never visited them. When her friends were gone she would resume to her role of the firm authoritarian.

Thakuma loved to listen to the radio when she would go to bed, calling the day off. In her bedroom everything smelled of betel leaves, old perfume and floor polish. I loved the way she carried the ivory glow on her wheatish skin.

I've yet to meet someone like her with infinite dominance. She displayed pride over the fact that all her six children were brought up under her strict discipline and guidance. Her confidence and ego was her beauty and that made Thakuma my Thakuma...a special granny.

And why I'm writing her account here? Because her golden rings remind me of her now...because I realised why she gave the earrings to me...that she wanted me to take her role in my father's life...love him like she did in her own special way.

It may feel strange but I get immense comfort from little things used by Thakuma. Just using her old cutting knife that she used to cut apples makes me feel close to her again. My house is now full of old fashioned, outdated objects from her life – things that tell me who I am through who she has been. The earring takes me into a land of fading clouds...clouds of memories which are so largely dominated by not the most expressive kind of grandmas I know, Thakuma.

19

Aberration

'Love? Honesty? You get all such things in the next world, in this world you've got to fight to make your own place,' Maya switched off the television and stood stiff, facing Sanjay.

'I think our soup is ready. Let me get it here.'

'Wait and listen to me. I'm almost certain of an affair and believe me when I say so. I've seen marks of lipstick on his collar, a couple of times,' her eyes widened in anguish as she continued, 'I've heard him take Sameera's name in his sleep. The whole idea is not only outrageous, but unthinkable too. I feel like a rat in the trap. Why in hell did I have to age and look pretty no longer? Why? Lately, you know, I've had nightmares of that bitch.'

Sanjay took off his spectacles, the rims of which had been forming a sharp impression on his nose. 'A nightmare?'

Maya rushed back to her seat, eager to speak out everything that had been troubling her. 'Yes, last night. From what I could understand, it was one of the winter months, precisely, towards the end of winter. My husband went to stay at a private villa in Nainital, and he chose to spend time with Sameera in that disturbingly romantic place...and not me.'

'Oh yes, the private villa. That reminds me about our plans. Did you give it a thought?'

'How could I forget what I saw? They went to the Emily Villa, I clearly remember the name,' Maya creased her brows as she tried to recall, ignoring what Sanjay just said, '*The Emily Villa.* Everything was set in the theme of the Colonial era in the early 20th century, everything – the furniture, the tea cups, even the people working there were dressed like the British.'

'You must be crazy, Maya. Even on this date, you've got a place resembling the Colonial era! Have you been watching or reading too much of fiction lately? Or do you still remember those days so well? It's worth a praise.'

'You believe me or not, the villa was beautiful, simply beautiful, in the midst of the lush green oak forest on the Ayarpatta slopes. I've always wanted to visit a place like this...and have my own pretty moment with him. Sameera stole it from me!'

'Maya, forget it, only know that you love him a lot and he loves you. Yes, I love you. You're such a lovely person and we all love you!'

Maya looked away and continued, 'Yes, I love him. But who knows what happened for real? Besides, I really feel, there is some connection. There must be...or why is it that he was so close to Sameera? I remember everything, there wasn't even a tiny bit of space between them, left for me. I've always loved him so much you know and this is what he does to me.'

'Okay Maya, look here, at me,' Sanjay urged, 'tell me more.'

'Sameera, that woman, she was wearing a gown...an impeccably white gown, like the one I always wanted for myself. They were sitting inside the hall and having tea...it was Yorkshire tea, you know, the famous Yorkshire tea. And then they took a walk around the house. They were holding hands. Bull shit! I want to kill her. But that sure is a cold-blooded way to look at it and my blood is anything but cold at the moment. I know I'm hot with fury and agitation. I can't keep still. I'll have to look for a way out.

Any way.'

'You're going through a lot of stress, Maya. I can understand. It must be really terrible. I've got to ask you one thing, how're you so sure the man was your husband? It could've been somebody else! It could be Sameera's husband!'

'Oh that bitch is unmarried, and remains so to torture me. I still can't recover from the shock. Somewhere, deep within, I knew the man couldn't be my husband. I tried very hard to look for little things in the man to prove that it wasn't him. But the resemblance was so strong and his habits so fixed...he looked so familiar and I was inclined to trust it was him. It was him. Else, what was she doing there?'

'And how're you sure about the woman? Have you met her before?'

'Ah! Many times! In the office parties, she usually stands at one dark corner of the hall; with those seducing eyes of hers she keeps eyeing at my husband. And occasionally gives me a look. She has that little something which, I know, men love. Men are all the same.' Maya paused for a while and continued, 'She is Sameera. I called her by that name once and she looked at me. The same girl was with my husband. Sameera.'

'And what else did the two do inside the villa?'

'So they walked around the house. One step brought them into the sitting room, without any introductory passage or lobby. I think it was called Emily's Lounge. The floor they walked on was made of stones – the chairs, high backed, primitive structures, painted biscuit brown. I must say, the architect had done a splendid job, the narrow windows were deeply set in the wall and the corners defending with large jutting stones. And then they went to the coziest part of the house that splendidly reflected both heat and light. And as the wind moved over the edge of the excessive slant of a few stunted trees at the front end of the villa, they engaged in a warm kiss, followed by aggressively undressing each other. And then I woke up in the hours before dawn, trembling and stiff with terror. The abrupt plunge into reality was equally scary.'

'I'm there for you, Maya...I've always been. Look, you're getting late for breakfast now.'

'What the hell is going on between my husband and that bitch?' Maya's patience was at its lowest ebb and she was ready to burst.

Sanjay knew that she was serious. 'Look, Maya. There is nothing going on between the two of them. Just a little bit of healthy flirting, I'd say.'

'Flirting? Healthy flirting? Really Sanjay...' she rolled her eyes in disgust. 'That's what you men call it? There is nothing healthy about flirting, Sanjay, not for a married man. Healthy flirting is a term introduced by perverted men who want to lend legitimacy to their extramarital dalliances. Flirting invariably has a sexual connotation to it.'

She got up from her seat and walked around the room gesticulating and muttering something to herself. Suddenly she stopped, turned back, looked at Sanjay and asked, 'Did my husband sleep with her? You are his friend. Did he ever tell you anything about it?'

Maya covered her face with her hands which couldn't stop the tears from rolling down. 'Why did he do this? Why?' she kept murmuring. The minute wrinkles on her cheeks shone in the light of the sun that entered through the window. Sanjay walked towards Maya and gently placed his hands on her shoulders.

'And this time, Maya, you really missed that part, where

you'd speak of going back to the times that wasn't measured by cuckoos that sprang out of clocks.' The sound of a door creaking with the wind brought her out of the trance. Maya looked up. He reached out and took her hands between his own. The corner of her lips trembled as she stared at his deep set eyes between the sharp fanning wrinkles on the thin skin. He jerked her shoulder gently and continued, 'Look I'm here, we're here, and there's no Sameera.'

Maya kept looking into his eyes for long. She walked back to her seat and sat down. 'But haven't I aged?'

Sanjay came swiftly over to where Maya was seated and sat down beside her. Before Maya could say something more than to register the extraordinary look of speculative assurance on the face of her psychiatrist husband, he said, 'You're still the most beautiful woman in that white gown, Maya. And I can picture you walking around the Emily Villa, holding my hands, like we did fifty-three years ago.' Sanjay looked down at her, moving his hands over her head and smiled. 'And that cozy part of the villa, still, is our pretty place, yes!' Maya's mouth fell open and remained like that for a while.

'Let's visit Nainital again. The Emily Villa. The Colonial era. How about this January?' Sanjay said and silently stood up and walked towards the kitchen to get Maya's soup bowl. Maya kept waiting at the dining table.

She closed her eyes and the wrinkles on her face deepened as her lips curved into a smile. She went back to the time when her curious fingers ran through the old and crumbling pages of the books kept in the huge wooden cupboard at the corner of the sitting room of the Emily Villa. Sanjay kept himself busy clicking photos and capturing her flawless serenity. Her white gown effortlessly merged in the Colonial setting. There was a smooth transition, at the end of which Maya noticed her fingers creasing fast, resembling the furrowed pages of the book that she was holding. She touched her face, her skin did not feel either smooth or supple. Very desperately, Maya turned around. The love in his eyes remained absolute and unchanged, just like the flawless white gown she was still wearing. Sanjay had aged too, but he remained the handsome psychologist husband as ever. So do I too look pretty in his eyes, she thought. She took a deep breath and opened her eyes. She was still smiling.

At the end of the story of her nightmare which he had been listening to patiently over the years, every day, they enjoyed their breakfast in a silence that was sometimes punctuated by the noise made by the spoon and sometimes by the gushing wind...the story that was structured out of Maya's delusion of irrational beliefs which she held with so much of conviction. And each time it was love that won over any kind of nightmare.

20

The Scent of Honeysuckle

I was always very fond of my mother's maternal uncles, aunts and cousins. My grandmother spent most of her childhood in a small town called Chakdaha in the Nadia district of West Bengal. When I was in school, every year I spent a month of summer vacation in their Chakdaha house. I think I was more attached to my mother's cousins than my own. And I simply adored the company of my second cousins. Over the years, I had formed this habit of taking long walks through unfamiliar roads in their company. It had been eight years now that I've started living in Mumbai with my parents and last month, after a long gap of nine years, I visited Chakdaha again.

This visit was unlike the regular ones I made years ago. My cousins have all grown up and most of them do not live there any longer. My grandmother is no more, and this was my first visit to her paternal home after her demise. My mother's uncles were still living in that house. I had it strongly set in mind that I would get to see a different Chakdaha this time.

It was towards the end of the rains and I was a little taken aback to see the trees and the fields as alive as years back. Nothing had really changed. The strange, pretty birds were still chirping on the branches – the beautiful pigeons in shades of black, white and grey, blue jays, weaver birds and kingfishers. The green and gold parrots too were dazzling. The ponds or jheels were all there with the ducks – as graceful as ever.

The people of Chakdaha were still simple in their ways. The cycle rickshaw was the best way of getting about the place. The rickshaw stand was just outside the railway station and one such stand appeared in every two kilometers. As a child I had always been fascinated by rickshaws – bringing in air from every direction. I was glad to see the smooth sliding movement and sluggish rate of motion of scores of rickshaws on the main road the rickshaw driver juggling his way through the marketplace – I really miss them in Mumbai – I was happy to see them alive here. The drivers looked at me, my heart wanted to climb onto one. However, I decided to wander in the familiar streets before I took a rickshaw to my grandmother's paternal house. I walked past shops gleaming with fine art work on wood or sweets piled high as the shopkeepers nodded drowsily.

The vegetable store had always been the most happening part of the market place. Down the road, near the Netaji Subhash Chandra Bose statue, the grocery store was still run by the widow. I remember she sold rice, pulses, spices – everything except vegetables and meat. It was the biggest grocery store in the place. It was rather famous for this woman. I had always regarded her as a strong lady since I had once witnessed her fighting with a man. She was known to fight in public with anybody who tried to get the better of her. However, she was a very convincing saleswoman and she knew all the little tricks of persuasion – overall, a great business woman. I was pleased to see her temperament on the high after so many years.

I walked up to the Krishna Temple near one of the ponds. The sky was crowded with bright paper kites – fluttering effortlessly in the cloudless sky. I could not remember seeing so many kites before. I recalled the days when I learnt to fly a kite here. The sun was beating down, striking the golden marble of the temple producing a lot of dazzle with the reflected light I was temporarily deprived of sight. I averted my eyes. Soon a small cloud – very small – covered the sun and I could look at the temple in the softened light. I walked towards the gate. Street vendors occupied the pavement, lest their competitors should take advantage of their absence. The old banyan tree stood there at the entrance – a kite was entangled in the upper most branches. It had always been the only tree in the street, growing out of the temple wall – all and straight. The pigeons had found a place under the shed of the tree. There were honeysuckles growing along the trunk – he bicoloured tubular flowers of the shrub widely distributed its fragrance throughout the place.

I reached the base of the banyan tree and was about to open the gate when all of a sudden I could feel a pair of hands touch my feet. I quickly looked at the ground and saw a feeble woman sitting against the tree, wearing a thoroughly torn and worn out printed cotton sari. She looked extremely skinny and unhealthy.

'How can I help you,' I said, bending down.

'I haven't eaten anything since the last three days,' she replied, 'please give me some water.' Her broken voice was extremely weak. I took out my water bottle. The woman dropped most of the water on her. Her hands were shaking continuously.

'Where do you stay?'

She nodded her head and said, 'I've come here from Bangladesh. And I've nowhere to go – they would've traded me off.'

I looked at her closely. She must have been in her early twenties but looked a lot older.

'Bangladesh? How have you crossed the border?'

She looked at me with her fainting eyes and said, 'The rivers by the boat...Midnapur.' I was a little offended by her reply. This is a serious problem in our country – the problem of migration of refugees, I thought, endless flow of migrants create sociopolitical, communal and economic tension throughout the state.

'They wanted to sell me,' she continued, looking away. She had no tears in her eyes. She looked dehydrated, she needed water, I thought. I walked up towards the temple gate and reached the place where there used to be a hand pump. There was a water tap system in place and I quickly filled my bottle and rushed towards the woman.

'Here,' I said giving her the water bottle, 'drink slowly this time.' She took the water bottle from me. I noticed wound marks all over her hands. It was quite evident that she escaped a close death in her country. She finished the water from the bottle and looked much more at ease. 'God bless you. Thanks a lot,' she said. Her voice appeared much better this time.

'I did nothing. Don't thank me, it was just water. What's your name and tell me what happened to you, what do you mean by being sold?' I insisted.

'I'm Ramia. My uncle and aunt – they've sold me.'

'To whom? This isn't legal.'

'To an old merchant. He wanted to use me in his business.'

'What kind of business?'

'It's a dirty business. It's the trade of flesh. He wanted me to do all that with man.'

'But how did your parents allow your uncle and aunt to do this?'

'They would've never let this happen, I'm sure. I'd lost my

parents – both of them – in my childhood. Since then I'm living with my uncle.'

'Are you aware this is human trafficking – it is illegal? Why didn't you complain to the police?'

The air moved her dry and dull hair as she turned to face me, 'But why would the police listen to me?'

'Why would your uncle and aunt do such a thing? They'd been taking care of you for years. Why all of a sudden?'

'I grew up not knowing who my parents are,' she said looking away. 'I did all the household work for my uncle and aunt since then. They'd beat me every day. Lately, my uncle started molesting me. When I complained to my aunt, she started whipping me with a belt and said that I would be sold off. Four days back they told me to pack my bags since I'd be going to a new home. I overheard their conversation from behind the door that I was sold. I'm aware. This is, I know, against the law to come here. But where else would I go? This was the way I could disappear and never be found. '

As I listened to her story I started feeling a slight sickness in my stomach. It was getting late. Everyone must be waiting for me at home, I thought. I picked up my bag to leave when she said, 'Will you please give me something to eat?'

The shops had all closed down by then and it would take at least three hours for those to reopen. I had a half-eaten sandwich inside my bag. I quickly took it out and offered her. She said at once, 'We can share it.' Those words kept ringing in my ears again and again.

I called a rickshaw from the end of the street. The leisurely pace of the gliding motion let me hold her gaze for a long time till she faded with distance. The birds were chirping, the kites were crowding the sky – but in the last one hour I had a great deal of realization about our hypocritical society.

It's been a month now and I'm back in Mumbai. The busy streets have no scope for cycle rickshaws. The sky has no space for fluttering kites. The chirp of pretty birds cannot penetrate through the noise of the traffic.

Recalling my grandmother's house, I feel it outlasted the others in the neighborhood for years since it was well maintained. Most of the houses, I had known, had to be rebuilt. The windows stood the same, only yellowed by time. I think the house still looked like the miniature castle from fairy tales. The elders had all turned old with time. I spoke a lot to them about life in Mumbai and how I despised it. I cannot recall anyone remembering my grandmother.

And while I think of my latest visit to one of the most remarkable places I've known, the memory of the Krishna Temple and Ramia remains deeply carved in my mind. I'd left her under the banyan tree shed – the coolest place nearby. Her story had undoubtedly moved me to an extent that I often dream about her. It was more than once I'd dreamt that I was Ramia – the girl who wanted to run away from reality – from everything that was expected – to a world that was more comfortable – though there were blockages in between the biggest of them all were called law, order and society. I'd always yearned to live in my grandmother's house – forever.

And just before I go to sleep, I look outside my window. Amidst the Mumbai streets, the traffic and the pollution – the air brings in the scent of honeysuckle from miles away, across the familiar streets of Chakdaha from the Krishna Temple with a bizarrely recognizable freshness – the outlandish scent in which Ramia, the woman who had nothing to give me, uttered the words, ‘We can share it.’

21

Choices in Mumbai

Last night I didn't get much sleep. I usually don't when I've worked abundantly and after a seventy-two hour shift at the fire station I intensely needed some clean air. So I woke up early in the morning and walked out of my small apartment to grab the morning freshness. Taxis made out of all kinds of cars were queued by the Mumbai-Pune Expressway.

I enjoyed the escape from my uniform and the dust and smoke that my job brings upon me by indulging in a brightly printed light cotton T-shirt and trousers, totally suited for a casual walk to the grocery store. Not that I had planned to do a lot of shopping; my thoughts ran more on the lines of sleeping late in the night and waking up early in the morning, and walking down the city.

I have a beautiful wife who insists every day that I should leave my job, which she considers to be tough and "not worth it". Sarita doesn't live with me in my small apartment. She lives in her parent's house in Pune...not that they have a big bungalow of their own. She is five-months pregnant.

Once in every month I visit my wife in Pune at their Chinchwad house. Of course, I am very excited about the little member who will soon become part of our family. The feeling is just amazing. But lately, I think I love the journey to Pune, the changing landscapes, when the bus reaches the point where the sun just drops and everything turns orange, when I become one with the wind, I love that more than the joy of seeing my wife.

In the early months of our marriage, it was difficult to maintain the proper mood for lackadaisical romance with the local sweeper industriously using his broom outside our door.

'That must be the dirtiest part of land in the entire city,' Sarita observed one morning as we lay in our bed listening to the ferocious noise of the broom.

'Perhaps we should've taken the third floor rooms. They're surely bigger than this one and we can have long, uninterrupted sleep there.'

'What's the point? This part of land doesn't seem any dirtier than your uniforms you bring back from your shifts, though.'

And without discussing it, I think we both felt that my job is despicable. My job gives me decently enough to have a roof over our heads, a comfortable place to establish our marriage, in a city as expensive as Mumbai, where they say finding God is easier than a place to stay. I have always suffered from reticence whenever our discussions arrived at switching jobs. However, I think after the long shift got over last night I'd reached the point where I couldn't take the cons of my job any more. So on the morning of a Monday, with nothing much to do, I decided to look out for some glittering prospect that Mumbai might have in its list of good jobs to offer me. I was feeling thoroughly determined.

People generally praise the weather of Pune...neither hot nor cold...an all-time spring settles over it. However, I find a mystery in the Mumbai rains. It wouldn't let you guess when it is coming, it won't tell you when it is tired of falling. The sun takes leaves for hours before it gets bored of staying idle. One can almost see the pollutants in the air. But what's strange is that despite of all the problems that we face we do nothing about it. We feel the threat of terrorists, bombers and terror attacks every moment, yet ignore everything in our mind. We are lively in fears of death simply because of the choices we make here. I sometimes see terrible things in the streets. I hate it when I see the greedy eyes of men by the station looking at the mother of four, as she moves from car to car describing her destitution; their wickedness in expecting the two-year-old little girl in her arms to grow up fast so they can extend their hands towards her. We read about such men in the newspapers, we see them in every second lane, but we choose to ignore them. Mumbai is all about the choices that we make every day. If the auto driver is unwilling to take you from Sion Circle to Chunabhatti Station, you wouldn't argue further... you'll continue to move on under the bad sun, in the dirty air, on the filthy road. Finally, I'd made my choice, to change my job, to live better.

I kept walking along the empty road. The shops on the side opened, one by one. I walked into the grocery store, the one near Sion Circle. I like this one because of the occasional discounts they offer. Not just the offers though, I love it also because it is just a walk away from my place. The boy at the counter was having a deep conversation with an old man. The old man adjusted his glasses. He smiled and said, 'Listen son, I give you three tips for success – read something no one else is reading, think something no one else is thinking, and do something no one else is doing.' Gradually, his eyes assumed the fervid gleam of some fanatic lecturer as he continued.

I moved inside towards the soap and shampoo section. There wasn't any discount that day. I could hear the noise of a slight confusion coming from outside. The goods delivery truck driver seemed to be having an argument with someone.

Mumbai is a late starter. But once the day starts, there is vigor, zest, enthusiasm, everything that's to do with energy in its spirits. The city of dreams turns impatient and unruly with the always-in-a-hurry people. Brace yourself Mumbai, the day has begun and I hope you have good news in store for me, I thought.

I walked towards the packaged food section. Since my wife became pregnant I've been living like a bachelor and all that I need is packed milk, bread and eggs. Sometimes, though, I like having something different. Packaged and ready to eat foods are blessings for men like us. I finished my shopping and moved towards the counter. I took out my purse and paid the boy. The old man looked irritatingly at me for the interruption and resumed his advice on success.

As I was walking towards the exit door, I felt a pat on my back and a thick voice said, 'Sachin! You're Sachin right!'

'Ajay! You're here buddy?' Ajay is an old friend. We grew up together in the little filthy gullies of the southern part of the city and I was seeing him this morning after almost a decade. 'How have you been?'

'I'm doing well. I work near Dadar Station. I stay nearby. How are you? You don't seem to have changed the slightest. You live nearby?'

'I live with my wife here in this part of the city. Its two streets from the Sion Station. You're working in Dadar! What kind of work?'

'I've opened an agency. It provides employees on contract basis to designing companies. They do small jobs like typing stuff and getting them printed. The engineers design bridges, these contract workers from our agency get the prints.'

'Oh well. Ajay, I'm in desperately in need of a job. The current work is getting too hectic. I do not know if I have the skills required to work with you.'

'Here in my company all you need to know is typing, printing and looking professional. My agency will teach you all of that. C'mon you're my friend, I can do this bit.'

'I don't have the slightest idea how I should thank you. You're being such a help in this moment of crisis. Come over sometime for tea.'

We exchanged mobile numbers and I thanked him for my new job.

'I will come to your place today?' I said.

'See you today at 11 then.'

I looked at him as he walked towards the vegetable section of the store. I smiled to myself. I carefully folded the paper in which Ajay wrote the address of his office and kept it inside my shirt pocket.

I came out of the store and waited for the signal to turn red. The sky looked like it would rain. I don't like to use subways, particularly in the monsoons. The rain water lies in small circular patches. And when it's almost twenty-four hours of moderate rainfall, mosquitoes and flies fill a large part of the space making the place stink terribly.

I seldom questioned myself about my decision to stick to my job in a city where choices are many, opportunities come every second step that you take. I have no idea why I'd never given this a serious thought before. I'm glad that I did now. Sarita, I knew, would be particularly happy and I could hardly wait to give her the news. I've always adored the idea of giving her surprises.

I was looking at the traffic signal when all of a sudden, I heard someone speeding towards my direction. I looked towards my right. A woman ran up to me at the store entrance and gave me a hug. I tensed up and she let go with tears of joy in her eyes so I could see her. She was a middle-aged lady in a blue cotton salwar suit. She was very fair and had a lot of jewellery on her. She was pretty. I tried hard to remember her face but I couldn't recognize her.

'Madam, pardon me, I think you're mistaking me for someone else.'

'On 26th November 2008,' she said with the most sincere smile I've known, 'you carried me out of the Taj Mahal Palace Hotel. All of a sudden there were explosions in the hotel, massive noise of what certainly I thought was gunfire. I don't remember anything after that. I was lying there on the floor for hours before you carried me!'

26th November was the story of the most audacious and devastating terror attacks in recent years...it showed the resilience of the city which had no choice but to proceed with life. I remember that it was my weekly off day. I received a call towards the evening and had to rush to the biggest hotel in the city. It was difficult. I was a little scared but back then I took everything as a challenge. I had no wife to take care of then.

I awkwardly smiled back at her. 'You're one of the heroes of the city, the nation. You save lives. God will bless you in abundance,' she said and walked inside her big car. I couldn't make out which car it was but it showed that it was worth a lot of money and she looked affluent.

Beneath all the terror and all the hatred and all the figures of lives lost remain these little experiences which give fire fighters like us the will to move on...the choice that we make here, in Mumbai. I got the answer to my question, to why I never felt the urge to change my job before.

The signal turned red. I was just about to cross the road when I realised that I forgot to get powdered detergent for my uniforms that got dirty. I turned around and walked briskly inside the grocery store.

22

The Enlightened Eyes

(An adaptation from
Rabindranath Tagore's poem, Upagupta)

Through the long, mundane years of my childhood, sometimes when I thought of my parents who had abandoned me at birth, I would run to Kamala *Masi* and tighten my grip around her slender waist and ask for a story. She would imprint a kiss on my forehead and excusing herself from the girls, she would take me inside the ashram foyer. It was a large hall facing the slopes covered with lush green oak trees, lit by the golden sunlight that made its ways through the windows with patterns drawn around the edges. The girls made fresh patterns once in every seven days with rice powder mixed in water. The air carried the sweet smell of jasmine flowers from the hills.

Kamala Masi knew many wondrous tales ranging from history to mythology. But on days when I recalled my blurry past, she knew the story that would keep me calm. I think I enjoyed listening to it so much because it made me feel wanted and loved. In those times, when Kamala Masi would be busy teaching the art of dance to her girls, I would find very few things that made me feel required. And this story did. Now I believe even Kamala Masi knew this and hence, even though she had other things to do, she wouldn't mind narrating the story over and over again. I would sit cross-legged on the floor that was studded with little stones. She would, very swiftly yet artfully, tie her hair into a bun that made her sharp features sharper, eyes bigger and darker – like the enchantress she told me about from her tales – take her seat on a high-backed chair and say, 'I was sitting alone near the oldest of all the oak trees, in a silence that was most familiar...that was sometimes punctuated by the howling birds or the gushing wind.'

She drew the small box of betel nuts nearer on the table made of thick wood, adjacent to her chair and continued while she cut the nuts with the cutter.

'It was time for the king's visit and I had to return to the ashram and dress myself in the best way I could. And then the storm came before the clouds covered the sky. The thunder frightened the birds away and I stood up to run back to the ashram.'

I watched her beautiful and glossy fingers moving swiftly as she began to narrate my favorite part of the story.

'The trees moved to and fro,' her lips, reddened by the betel nuts, continued, 'and a thick voice spoke amidst the rustling of the leaves – This evening, the king has been stopped by the storm. What waits for you at your abode is an abandoned baby girl, born from the womb of a celestial nymph, destined to meet your destiny. Teach her all you know.'

If I am destined to meet Kamala Masi's destiny would I take over the ashram and teach the art of dance to the girls, I thought, if anything, I wouldn't be harsh to them when they made the slightest mistakes. I'd give them a lot of leisure time which they'd use as they pleased and we would play all day.

'Where are you lost?'

'I was thinking. Didn't you ask more about my mother?'

'I guess the storm said what it had to. I thought in my mind I would call the baby girl Vasavadatta which means a gift.'

'But wasn't I abandoned by my mother? My name should've been something like *Lakshanabhrashta* or ill-fated, shouldn't it?'

'But you're destined to meet my destiny, remember? Kamala was desirable by everyone, so will be Vasavadatta.'

'Did the king visit you that evening? Did you dance?'

'He did come that evening. And he was blinded by the glow that radiated out of your little form; a golden gleam filled the place. He declared my successor, the next chief dancer for his son.'

'Why his son?'

'The old king who visited me years ago is dead. His son has taken the throne since a decade now. You, my dear, will serve his son, the king.'

I wondered several times since childhood...why was Kamala Masi always so mysterious about the dancer, or the chief dancer, or whatever she was to the king, and I was destined to be? However, I was the closest thing she had to a daughter and that infused a sense of responsibility inside me to become whatever she wanted me to be and also to be successful at it.

'Did it bother you...the fact that you had me to take care of?'

'I understood the law of nature. Beauty would soon fade away and the king would lose his interest in me before long. There would be wrinkles all over my face. I needed someone by my side and you came to me like a blessing.'

I didn't pay Kamala Masi's words on beauty much attention. I looked at a streak of grey hair over her ears. With the conceit of youth I thought I had years to go before I gave the process of ageing a careful study.

'How did I look like as a baby? Remember?'

'I have it very clear before my eyes till this day. The storm stopped and I reached home. Your colour as striking as gold lit the room with its shimmer, the eyes were longing for love and the lips, yearning for food. I took you in my arms when your tiny fingers, like the petals of a plumeria flower, brushed against my face. I visualized you learning dance with the other girls here. A year from now you'll have completed sixteen years on earth and the king will come to see you dance. You'll impress him with the moves I've taught you through the years. There'll be lust in his eyes and longing in his heart and then he'll come very often.'

I don't think I knew what either lust or longing meant then but the thought of everything else that she said was welcoming.

'How often, Masi?'

'Well, if you can do everything I teach you who knows, he might build a fort for you beside the palace.'

'A fort, for me! Like the one my mother lives in?'

✦

My legs would hurt for days. Everyday Kamala Masi made us practice the half seated posture, keeping my torso perfectly erect bending the knees sideways, since I was about three years. She called it the Araimandi. I understood its significance only when I was seven.

Kamala Masi made a face. Hitting me hard on my leg with her thick wooden stick she said, 'Bend them more.' Tears gathered at the corners of my eyes but Kamala Masi was stern when it came to dance.

With a score of other girls, some of my age and some elder to me, I stood in the front row, under the sun, in the soreness. Kamala Masi sat down on the chair under the shed of an oak tree and declared, 'This, girls, is the basic posture of dance.'

If I am struggling with the basics, how was I ever to meet Kamala Masi's destiny, I wondered.

'This? The basic posture?'

'Every mother and child relationship starts with the connection of the navel. This is said to be the connection that gives life, the star of selfless love.'

I looked down at the pretty little round that showed in the space between my blouse and skirt. I touched it. My fingers went around it and a strange shiver ran down my spine. I was satisfied I had been connected with my mother through this.

'Hands on your waist and sit down, shoulders straight,' Kamala Masi shouted, her teeth sparkled between the wrinkles at the ends of her lips, 'keep the distance between the head and the navel, and the navel and the ground same, so that the centre of this posture is the navel.'

The sun was getting warmer with every passing moment. With no sign of clouds or storm or rain we continued *Taiya-Tai* movements in the *Araimandi* position.

Kamala Masi was strict but I enjoyed the special privileges she let me enjoy over the other girls who stayed with us inside the ashram. They came to learn dance from Kamala Masi for sometimes a year, two years, five years or even more. During their tenure they cleaned the ashram, learnt needle craft, planted trees and cooked meals apart from dancing. At the end of their stay they returned to their homes. All that I was required to do was to learn dance and practice as much as I could. I regarded this as being lucky, though at times I was tired of the anklets tinkling all day. There were times when I wanted to plant a tree and take good care of it all by myself. Not that I had never tried planting one, and how could I ever forget the scolding I received from Masi after such an act. But I always had my reasons for loving her.

'Why Vasavadatta,' she said that night, sitting by my bed, before I fell asleep, 'do you have to do things I tell you not to? These...these pretty hands...the beautiful fingers are not for playing clumsy with mud and soil. They are for the dance mudras. What if you get some disease of the soil pests? Prepare yourself for a much royal cause you're born for.'

'Am I not born to be destined like you? Are you royal? What is it like being royal, Kamala Masi?'

She raised her eyebrows and looked outside the window that was opened by the air flowing through the door on the other end of the room. 'If you're born a girl, you can be royal if your father is a king. You can be royal if your husband is a king. There is another way you can be royal. If you are desirable by the king, if the king selects you as the chief dancer and takes you to the palace...you're almost like a queen.'

'Which of these three made you royal, Kamala Masi?'

'The king sent his men to take me to his palace every night. They would bring a new palanquin made of gold, studded with precious stones – the emeralds, the ruby – stones I had never seen, never heard of. And then I reached the palace. There would be the queen, green with jealousy. But the king would have his eyes set on me and I'd dance.'

'You made the queen jealous! That's way more than the queen's royalty.'

'Oh it was way more. And if you could please the king, each

day he would shower gold and jewelry on you till you were satisfied,' she turned towards me, on her way from her royal past, and said, 'the new king has taken the throne and people say that he's building a fort for a dancer. He would come for you.'

'And I'd get all that gold and jewelry and stay in the fort!'

'You'll not get any closer to royalty if you play with soil. A dancer should know how to make the art flow through every part of her body. You must take care of yourself.'

'Masi, I will make the queen jealous with my dance and beauty when I grow up.'

✦

I sat stubbornly under a mango tree in our garden, trying to concentrate on, as Kamala Masi would call it, the *Natya Shastra* or the text on arts.

Yato Hasta Stato Drishti
Yato Drishti Stato Manaha
Yato Manaha Stato Bhava
Yato Bhava Stato Rasa

Eyes follow the hands, followed by the mind and the feelings, to finally obtain the sweetness of the aesthetic bliss. It was a thick book that set out the fine art of dance that I had very little time left to master. The book described in conscientious, glum detail the different ways to mix *laya* with *tala* to bring out the perfect *bhava* and all the morose details made my eyelids drop. It was a summer morning and the deep golden petals of the daisy flower, radiating from dark brown centers, called me nearer. The fluffy golden yellow blooms atop tall stems moved gently in the slow breeze that travelled through the slopes. Insects joined with each other in a melodious chorus. The *krishnachura* petals or the flower of fire dropped lazily on the ground, carpeting it scarlet red. My escorts, other girls in the ashram, came looking for me. They, chewing betel leaf to redden their lips, murmured and giggled among themselves with little or no reasons. Forming a small canopy around where I sat, they gave me relief from the pitiless sun. I closed the book.

'Vasavadatta,' one of them said, 'Kamala Masi wants us to apply this turmeric paste mixed with yoghurt all over you.'

'You have to keep this on for almost an hour,' said another.

'She said it would make the skin glow and counter the ruinous effect of the sun.'

'Who knows, maybe you'll get married soon.'

'Where's Rasa,' I declared, 'I'll go only with her.'

✦

'I'm telling you this against Kamala Masi's wishes, Rasa,' I whispered into her ears. Rasa had been my companion since I was four. She was among the few girls who stayed the longest in the ashram. The ceiling of my room, a small and empty chamber facing the south showed the bare inside of a conical structure.

'What's it,' she asked as she applied the third layer of turmeric and yoghurt on my naked torso, 'that Kamala Masi doesn't want me to know?'

'The king had sent his messengers this morning. They were five of them in red uniform bordered with gold.'

'Did you see them, hear what they said? I hope there isn't a new problem, a war or theft or some new kind of disease.'

'No, nothing of that sort I must say. I overheard them speaking to Kamala Masi.' Very early in my childhood I had learnt to listen in. I was driven into doing this because the girls of the ashram never included me into their general discussions, jokes or gossips. I took to this immoral activity when I appeared to be sleeping or doing some dull work. Somehow I was close to Rasa. She was of my age and knew very little about the world outside the ashram, beyond the oak trees, mainly because she came here at a very small age. We enjoyed each other's company, discussing how the world outside this place would be, what the people did for a living, what the palace looked like.

'You saw the men?'

'Yes! I did see them,' I exclaimed in excitement. I had not seen many men in my life then, only the fathers of the girls when they came to bring them, visit them or take them from the ashram. 'They had thick voices, much thicker than any of us. They had short hair and two of them had hair on their faces. I think it's called the beard. Can you recall your father, Rasa.'

'Wait,' Rasa kept the bowl on the floor and looked at the wall and said, 'I have very feeble memories of him. Nothing that's very definitive. Oh Vasavadatta, I wonder when I go back home, if my parents, as I have imagined, would be happy to see me grown up. It's a matter of honor to have spent so many years in this ashram to the people outside.' She took some more mixture from the bowl and smoothly applied a layer on my neck that tickled slightly. 'Where would you go from here?'

'To the king, in the royal palanquin,' I said as I saw Rasa glaring into my eyes, half-closed, covered in a sweet day dream. I tried to hide my anguish of being born with no parents and continued, 'I heard one of them declaring to Kamala Masi that it's time that

Vasavadatta be sent to the palace. I had, through all the years, been waiting for this day, for the king to come. I am even more excited, you know why...they will take me to the palace. I'll get to see the world outside, for the first time. They said that someone called *Rajababu*, who would himself examine me. I don't know who he is, but I can tell you, Rasa, I am so thrilled.'

'The King! He is popularly called Rajababu.'

'Stop! Rajababu, the king!' I repeated the words in my mind.

'Vasavadatta, why are they asking for you? I mean to say, there are others as well who would want to go, I'm sure.'

'Because I was destined to,' I think I said this with a slight hint of arrogance that made Rasa make a face at me as she wiped the yellow mixture off my body.

'Yes, maybe that's why Kamala Masi called us in an urgency giving us the bowl. Are you excited?'

'Of course I'm. Who knows, maybe I'll have a fort of my own. The floor made with marble stone, the walls carved out of crystal and the chandelier lighting the entire room all night.'

I noticed her envious eyes that filled me with ecstasy. For the first time in my sixteen years did I feel this way...a figure of jealousy, desired by the king, by Rajababu. I must be really very beautiful, I thought, as I held the mirror in front of me – glowing with the effect of turmeric and yoghurt.

✦

By the time I entered the hall Kamala Masi was already seated, her brows creased in a frown, and though she nodded, she didn't smile at me. I wanted to see what the king looked like. I thought it would be a wise idea and when I told this to Kamala Masi I could see the discontent on her face. I think it was troublesome for her to get the artist from the city to bring the king's picture.

The artist was setting up the paintings. There were five huge canvas stands carrying them, covered by a silk veil. They were almost the size of the windows that covered the front wall. He hadn't touched the tamarind juice that Kamala Masi had kept on the table beside him. He wore a turban on his head which he kept on the floor to let the sweat that dropped from his forehead dry in the soothing wind. The pitiless sun made his skin pitch black that glistened with moisture. The grey hair near the temples on his forehead and his bent posture made him look old.

I'd wished Rasa was there with me. I had always found greater ease when it came to talking about men with Rasa than with Kamala Masi. But she was nowhere to be seen. Perhaps, I thought with much displeasure, she was with the other girls enjoying luscious mangoes that lazily dropped on the ground.

I stared at the silk veil – wishing to know a thousand details – things that a potential chief dancer needed to know – beyond what the artist would show through his painting.

The artist unveiled the first painting. 'This is the noble king... our Rajababu,' he said. I stepped closer to it. His face was good humored and the crown on his head befitted the structure of his face perfectly. He did not smile but I could easily see through the corners of his lips a tiny lurking smirk. His eyes looked straight at me; I could see an outlandish intoxicating glance which was so bizarre that it kept visiting my restless mind. There was something in the eyes; maybe that's what Kamala Masi calls lust when he first mentioned him. Bedecked in jewels, he occupied the throne that was encrusted with gems. *Kuwarji*, I decided in my mind, I'd call him. I closed my eyes and pictured him on the throne, praising me.

'Open your eyes to the competitors you have, Vasavadatta,' Kamala Masi said, 'for you must know them well.'

The artist uncovered the other paintings. They were of a woman, all of them. 'But Masi, I wanted to see the king, who's she? A competitor, by what means?' I asked in distaste, 'She's much older to me. She wears jewels but they cannot hide the skin near her forehead that's beginning to crumple!'

Kamala Masi looked at the artist and nodded at him, signaling him to leave the hall. He picked up his turban and walked briskly towards the exit and waited outside. She stood up from her seat and walked towards me. 'This,' pointing at one of the paintings, she said, 'is the queen of this land, Maharani Vishakha. I ordered these paintings of the Maharani especially for you. Look at her, Vasavadatta. What went wrong that the king has called for you? Think!'

One of the paintings was older than the rest. In it, the queen looked pretty and girlish. Her curly hair fell over her forehead and she looked lost. This picture must've been taken before she married the king, I thought. 'Maybe she can't dance. Maybe she has forgotten all the steps! That's that reason she wants a dancer.'

'What he wants is a chief dancer. That's beyond what simply a dancer does. After everyone leaves the court and the chief dancer has concluded her dance, the king remains. He then spends the night with a chief dancer like he would with his queen.' Kamala Masi took a deep breath and continued, 'It seems you've got a lot to learn still. You're young, beautiful, and vivacious – things the queen has lost.'

That night Kamala Masi called me to her room. She rarely called me or other girls there, a small cabinet at the corner of the ashram, towards the north, led by the narrow passage from the hall. I think I had been to her room earlier only when she was not well. I learnt how the queen had shown great valor in her young years as a princess when her father was killed in a war and she had to fight against the king's enemies to save her kingdom.

I wanted to tell Kamala Masi how moved I was by the courage showed by the queen but I was forestalled by her. 'Don't,' she said with her cold eyes affixed upon mine, 'let your emotions make you weak, Vasavadatta. Understand why the king married her, what it takes to be royal and become a chief dancer.'

✦

One day I said, 'Tell me more about the chief dancer.'

I didn't think Kamala Masi would agree instantly, but she shrugged, 'It's time you learn all her roles. Go and quickly shut the door.'

I was beginning to feel weird about this kind of a clandestine lesson. I'd never say that Kamala Masi had ever neglected my education. Apart from dancing, she taught me singing and playing the veena. However, I enjoyed reading about the kings and queens and stories of their valor. As a child I never really took pleasure in dancing. This, I believe, was partly because I rarely realised what the steps and gestures meant and partly since I had always imagined that my celestial nymph mother had burdened me with dance. Hence, much before I was big enough to know the depth and the theories of dance I started taking my lessons as a forced obligation. I think growing up had transformed me and I started making sense of all that the storm had told Kamala Masi about my birth and I began thinking about dance as a good companion. And as she said, a million times since my birth, I was destined to be among the royals, my only goal was to step inside the palace and become the chief dancer. I was already burning from within with the desire to meet Kuwarji. I thought I was in love with him since that was exactly the kind of feeling that Kamala Masi had illustrated when she taught us Raga Hindol, the raga of love.

'The other day, I remember, you said the king remains after the others leave.'

'I've that in my mind. I'm going to tell you some new things and reiterate a few older ones.' She grinned. I was really interested to see what she had to offer.

'I hope I wouldn't have to dance all night. I wonder what would become of my feet.'

'A chief dancer cannot be so light hearted, Vasavadatta. I assure you wouldn't be told to dance all night, but there's something more. And remember, the king would expect you to know them.'

The king looked strict in the painting, I thought, though I had also noticed a hint of humor cornering the lips. I had decided the strictness was a humanly fault of the artist and let go of the contemplation. However, Kamala Masi's words made me rethink.

She laughed out loud and said, 'When you're done with the dance and the other men leave the room, the king will stay back. Be seated and give him a glance from the corner of the eye, like this, your brows slightly tilted and mischief at the corner of your lips.'

'Like in abhinaya, how lovers call each other, how Radha calls Krishna, is it?'

'Exactly and slightly more. If the king comes towards you, be seated. If not, start walking towards the side wall, swaying your hips,' she said demonstrating the walk and said, 'now that cannot stop the king from coming closer.'

'But I could've simply called Ku...I mean the king towards me. Isn't walking like that a little hilarious?'

She rebuked me sharply and said, 'You shouldn't ever be obvious with men. Men are always drawn towards mystery. Everything you do should have an enigma that he cannot resist to unfold. And when he comes close, take deep breaths. This will draw his mind towards your youthfulness.'

'But won't this be boring every day? How will it remain a mystery?'

'Absolutely, it is tough to keep up the king's interest through months and years. If you've got the variety, you've got it all. But the first night is always the most significant; it sets the fire on. Once it is set, you simply need to make sure that it continues to burn.' She lit the lamps in her room as it got darker outside. I noticed an intensity with which she spoke. I started to enjoy the conversation as it progressed. It was new.

'And when you're so close to him and you can feel his warm breath, bite his lower lip, slightly.'

'Now isn't this too obvious? Making this move, I mean the biting and all. Where's the mystery?'

'That's what I call is the correct blend of giving and receiving,' she replied as she lit the next lantern, 'a perfect lovemaking has the right mixture of both.'

✦

Rasa and the other girls murmured around me – sometimes smiling at and sometimes whispering to each other – as I kept sitting before Kamala Masi's mirror inside her room, towards the back end. It was a large piece of glass that made me seem important... like a battle armor, or more correctly, a bride. I was decked with heavy ornaments of gold and silver, my hair was being dried with the fumes of agarbatti or joss stick, the sweet smell of which quickly filled the room, while the others simultaneously applied pollen grains of red summer flowers on my cheeks. I saw Kamala Masi standing behind me from the mirror as the girls made way for her. I stood up and turned around.

She didn't utter a word but I saw her smile underneath those stern eyes. She looked pleased. She gently held the end of the blue and golden sari I was wearing and cleverly put it over my chest to draw attention to my breasts with a slight hint of the cleavage. With a clever smile she placed the joss sticks between my legs, on the floor, the fumes vigorously rushing upwards. She, then, rubbed rose water on my navel.

The palanquin was waiting outside, grand as it was, exactly like I had imagined it would be. Studded with precious stones it was glistening under the sunset sky. An insidious voice inside me said, do not be proud of all these that glitter before you... they could be a veil of glamour behind which lies a more perilous reality. I must be foolish, I thought, all this is actually happening like it's supposed to.

I made sure I hugged everyone in the ashram before leaving. I stood before Kamala Masi. Kissing my forehead, she said, 'Be a winner, child. May he not be able to lose you before his eyes, for even a minute. Go and live your life like the queen.' Her face was swollen with pride. I thought I was seeing Kamala Masi, the woman who was more than a mother, for the last time before long. My eyes were beginning to moisten. I did not expect the same from those firm eyes. But maybe because I was the closest one she had to a daughter, or because she sensed a deeper, darker future, or maybe because she, too, was saddened by our distance, I saw tears forming at the corners of her eyes that gently dropped down.

Inside the palanquin it was dark and fresh. It was covered with muslin cloth that moved with the air. I looked outside, amazed by the oak forest, feeling the air over my face. Thus began my life outside the ashram. Like an infant born out of her mother's womb I looked outside in curiosity and fear. What if the city of Mathura doesn't welcome me well, I thought. A sinister voice from inside urged me to go back to the life of comfort with Kamala Masi. But then, wasn't life in the palace supposed to bring me all the happiness in the world? Still, the voice constantly asked the rhetorical question...what if?

As the palanquin reached towards the forest exit, the city of Mathura received us. The carrier men, four of them, must be in a lot of pain, I thought. I imagined the agony they must have been feeling with each step on the cracked, rugged path through the forest. I saw a banyan tree by the road. For once I thought about asking them to rest, stretching their possibly throbbing feet under the shed. But it was getting darker and the king with his men was probably waiting for me and so I let the thought pass.

We went through a small marketplace. I knew this because that's what Rasa had told me marketplaces looked like. Men and women selling and buying fruits, vegetables, cloth, utensils and other things in small chambers which, I remember, she had described in detail and called them shops. Towards a corner there was a broken structure, covered in old, dried leaves and cornered by cobwebs. It was an old temple without a priest to ring a bell, without the sound of a conch shell. A puff of wind gushed across my face as I remembered the tiny temple beside our ashram. It scared me that I could not recall having visited it before stepping on the palanquin.

The palanquin slowed its pace. Across the road I saw the arched top of the palace. Though I'd heard a lot from Kamala Masi what the palace looked like, her words fired an eagerness to see it with my eyes, which, I thought, if I was lucky enough could be my new home. I had always pictured about a structure that would, in many ways, be in contrast to the ashram. Scented air would stream in through large windows and doors across hallways with liberal balconies. The palanquin stopped outside the gate of the palace.

Before my feet touched the ground red velvet was laid for me to walk my way to the palace. There were no light on the road, the doors were all shut. The starless murky sky of August looked like it was midnight. Commoners, holding little lamps, dressed in mediocre attire with little or no jewelry on them made way as I stepped outside. The guards at the palace gate, in thick red and black costumes, holding long and slender pointed weapons examined me. Their eyes were dripping with strangeness. Maybe that's what Kamala Masi said the look of lust looked like. This is my doorway to royalty, I said to myself. Smiling at the guards, with my lips slightly tilted and brows raised, I walked away. I could see the hallway from a distance. The walls were shimmering with gold and silver in the light of the moon. It overlooked a garden with colourful flowers which, I thought, must be celebrated by pretty butterflies and singing birds in the day. Sound of the veena made by deft musicians came from the palace. I kept walking, accompanied by few commoner women I saw at the gate. They walked silently.

Suddenly, I stepped back as I could feel my feet touching a person. I slowly lowered the lamp and saw a man, dressed like an ascetic, lying asleep in the dust. He woke up startled. I'd never seen such enlightened eyes before, radiating tons and tons of knowledge. 'Forgive me, young ascetic,' I apologized, 'and graciously come along with me. I'll request Kuwarji, the king, to give you a place in his majestic palace. The dusty earth, believe me, is not at all the bed you deserve!'

The young ascetic smiled at me in the most gentle way and politely said, 'Woman, please carry on. I promise to come to you when time is ripe.'

I smiled back and walked away from him. Just then, I fixed my glance at a ghastly structure, a statue erected at the center of a pond with the garden surrounding it. I had read in tales that kings often built such appalling structures outside their homes to keep away from bad omens. Must be so, I thought.

On the other end of the garden there stood another fort built with, what it looked in the mild moonlight, crystal pieces or blue glass. It was dark from inside, the windows were shut; it looked disturbingly silent unlike the main palace. Maybe that's the fort the king has built for me, I imagined. Unlike the times of Kamala Masi, the chief dancer gets a palace of her own. It was a strange feeling to see my dreams of so many years come true. I imagined my room at the top of the fort, washed by the fresh air. I would look at the entire city of Mathura from the balcony made with marble. If Kamala Masi had been with me, she would have at once known what I had been thinking and with a sharp rebuke she'd say, 'Everything worth having comes with a trial worth withstanding.'

I took the wide steps towards the hallway. The steps were covered by carpets that were too soft and my feet were almost sucked into them till my ankles. At the entrance I saw a statue of a dancing woman who looked like Kamala Masi. All of a sudden I yearned to be close to her and let her guide me through the trial. I wondered if she also wished the same.

The inside of the palace looked like an enigma. I'd never seen so much gold and silver on walls and swollen domes. The large door at the entrance of the hall was embellished with expensive metal and precious stones. Someone opened it and I walked inside to the center. There was too much light around.

I saw the king at a distance. I joined my hands and bowed as Kamala Masi taught me. The king raised his hands in a motion which, I thought, meant benediction. I longed to see the kings face closely. I was so thrilled that I feared the other spectators surrounding me would hear the beats of my heart. I wanted to know if the king was as good humored as the artist had portrayed. Instead, I focused on his torso; the powerful bare chest was calling me nearer to him. Kuwarji, I murmured, I will win your heart.

I could sense that all eyes were on me. I could hear small whispers around. The king's men were probably commenting about me, striking their knees and smiling slyly. The king was quiet. He gestured his hands and the music began.

✦

The other spectators left. In the huge hall, which could encompass a hundred giants, I sat still at the center. I kept my eyes on the floor, my face vigilantly impassive. I called all the gods I knew.

I strongly hoped that I'd won the test. The white petals of the flower garland on my head were beginning to wear. I saw few of them on the floor. I noticed carefully spaced steps approaching where I sat. I was about to show all my anxiety through my facial expressions. But this is what I am expecting – a thought came to my mind. I loosened the muscles on my face using the methods Kamala Masi had taught.

'What's your name, girl?' a heavy voice asked; I felt his warm touch on my forearms and I stood up.

'Vasavadatta,' I said as Kamala Masi had instructed, 'the desirable one.' I let go of his hands as I walked in little steps towards the side wall, carefully moving myself, accentuating the hidden pleasures and looking back at him I asked, 'What do you think?'

His laughter almost exploded the hall as he walked briskly towards me. 'Come with me, Vasavadatta.' He held my hand like a little impatient kid and we walked out of the hall, by the garden, towards the other fort. It somehow felt nice to be with him though we barely spoke. It was difficult to match his long steps. He's got childish whims, I thought. We rushed past the horrible statue on the lake and before long we reached the other fort. Scented with rose, decorated with lotus, the fort was smaller than the main palace but beautiful in its own way. As I kept walking, a magic air or chant or some out of the world power lighted the lamps and showed the passage. It led to a foyer that housed fountains and pools where birds played. Through the hallway we reached the stairs. The blue glass wall shone brilliantly in the light. We reached the topmost chamber.

It was serene. I turned around at the king. The dark brown eyes glittered. His smile called me nearer. 'Dear Vasavadatta,' he said, 'all the years I'd only heard about your beauty. I imagined you in my mind. But you're like a celestial woman. I've built this fort for you, Vasavadatta, a gift which could match your beauty. It seems a gift as such is impossible.'

I wondered if it was Kamala Masi who had told the king about me. Nevertheless, I was flattered by the king's remark.

I let the kiss linger on before lightly grazing my lips over his. As Kamala Masi taught me, I was sure this act had sent sparks down his spine making him crave for the passionate and rewarding end of the night. He spread out his arms and then tried to pull my face towards him. His lips were craving to satiate their thirst from my scented breath. He repeatedly whispered into my ears, 'Vasavadatta, the gift.' The veena played from the antechamber Raga Kedar, the raga of inner desire, accompanied by the tanpura.

We smiled at each other down leaving deep and exhausted air. Calmness ran through my body as I looked outside the window. The stars, the moon, the room, Kuwarji...everything was a hundredfold times more magnificent than I had dreamt. We laughed and giggled, as the queen probably wept in a dark corner in the palace.

✦

Three months later, I looked with my wailing eyes at the sunrays that seeped in between the leaves of the tall palm trees like little diamonds. The early spring flowers nodded in the calm air as if to suggest the much warmer summer days waiting. The morning dew drops on the delicate pansy petals have dried by now, showing the lilac shades bright and clear, and the marbled leaves of yellow trilliums quivered gently, making its delicate yellow-white blooms a welcome sight. The sun was shining and the artistically carved terrace edge of the palace that overlooked the garden formed a smooth tangent to its round surface. It is from here that the kings have radiated their power to decide the destiny of their subjects, both men and women, exactly the same way Kuwarji had decided my ill-fated prospect. And as I stared at the dark sores of disease on my hands, which he had given me and which had spread cruelly throughout my body, a couple of young boys in their late teens ran towards me with stones, one of which hit my forehead. As Kuwarji had ordered, I was supposed to move out of Mathura...I realised I should better hurry. I recalled Kamala Masi and longed to be with her. However, after years of nurture and upbringing it would be wrong to give her my poisonous contagion.

I stood up on my weak legs and tried to walk. I could see the statue – the most gruesome place inside this enormous citadel – just her hair, from outside the palace, under the old banyan tree across the road beside the remains of the dilapidated temple. The hideous female statue with snakes in place of her hair stands on a large painted rock at the center of a small artificial lake, with fountains bordering it. The beautiful and glistening blue-green peacocks, I thought, must be showing off the gorgeous green and blue feathers on its train, elongating their upper tail, taking rounds around the statue.

After a couple of steps, I lost balance and fell down on the dusty earth. My forehead was already bleeding and hurting badly. I was hungry and thirsty. I must be looking terrible now, I thought, such that no man would ever desire the once desirable

Vasavadatta.

The scorching rays of the sun were almost killing me when I felt tiny drops of water on my lips and gentle fingers smearing my body with sandal balm. It was soothing. I closed my eyes for some time as the pain began to subside.

'Who are you, merciful one?' I asked with my broken voice.

I tried to recall his face, but everything was blurry, except a pair of enlightened eyes. 'It's time at last, and I'm here,' he replied.

Debalina is an alumna of the 2015 batch of IIM Lucknow. She is the Critics' Choice Award winner of Illuminati '11, winner of the McGough & Co. International Letter Writing Competition and recipient of the winning award of Anubhuti '14 at the Lucknow Literary Fest. Her debut novel, *The Female Ward*, was internationally published in 2013. Debalina works as a management consultant. She also sings Rabindrasangeet, performs Bharatanatyam dance and enjoys public speaking.